"Climb up and let me check your stirrups."

Gabe made a step of his hands.

"I can check my own stirrups, and I don't need a boost." Belle climbed into the saddle in one easy motion. "They're fine."

"Good. The ground is rocky around here, so stick to the paths," Gabe said as he mounted.

They rode at a granny pace for ten or fifteen minutes—until Belle couldn't stand it anymore. She resettled the red hat on her head, yelled, "Race you!" and took off like greased lightning.

She glanced over her shoulder to find that Gabe was gaining fast. The mare wasn't a match for the big brute he rode, so she slowed, then pulled up.

"What the hell are you doing?" Gabe shouted when he stopped beside her and grabbed the reins.

Her eyes widened. "I beg your pardon?"

"You could have gotten yourself killed!"

"On a horse? I don't think so. With equal mounts, I could ride bareback and beat you any day of the week."

He glared at her for a minute, then his expression softened and morphed into a grin. "You probably could."

Dear Reader,

When I wrote the first three books about the Outlaw family of Naconiche, a fictitious small town in the Piney Woods of East Texas, I hadn't planned to write more about them. Folks seemed to enjoy the stories of the three older brothers who were all named for famous outlaws and all in law enforcement—J. J. (Jesse James) Outlaw in *The Sheriff*, Frank James Outlaw in *The Judge*, and Cole Younger Outlaw in *The Cop*—and I received lots of e-mail urging me to give the other two siblings, Belle Starr Outlaw and Sam Bass Outlaw, books of their own. I listened. This is Belle's book.

Belle, the only female among four brothers, was determined to succeed in law enforcement as well, so she aimed high and became an FBI agent. After a lot of soul searching, Belle rebelled against tradition and left the FBI. She married a Colorado rancher at the end of *The Cop*, but things went sour quickly. She heads back to Texas to find a new life and ends up in Wimberley, a picturesque little town in central Texas, where she meets her fate among another group of characters as colorful as those in Naconiche—and an angel of a hero. Wimberley is a real town, and you can check it out on the Web. They have real market days there as I've described, but if you go looking for the businesses and characters I write about, you won't find them in Wimberley. They're all figments of my active imagination. I hope you enjoy Belle's story.

To love and laughter!

Jan Hudson

THE REBEL

Jan Hudson

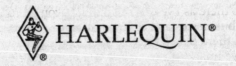

TORONTO • NEW YORK • LONDON
AMSTERDAM • PARIS • SYDNEY • HAMBURG
STOCKHOLM • ATHENS • TOKYO • MILAN • MADRID
PRAGUE • WARSAW • BUDAPEST • AUCKLAND

ISBN-13: 978-0-373-75139-6
ISBN-10:   0-373-75139-7

THE REBEL

ABOUT THE AUTHOR

Jan Hudson, a former college psychology teacher, is a RITA® Award-winning author of thirty books, a crackerjack hypnotist, a dream expert, a blue-ribbon flower arranger and a fairly decent bridge player. Her most memorable experience was riding a camel to visit the Sphinx and climbing the Great Pyramid in Egypt. A native Texan whose ancestors settled in Nacogdoches when Texas was a republic, she loves to write about the variety of colorful characters who populate the Lone Star State, unique individuals who celebrate life with a "howdy" and "y'all come." Jan and her husband currently reside in Austin, and she loves to hear from readers. E-mail her at JanHudsonBooks@gmail.com.

Books by Jan Hudson

HARLEQUIN AMERICAN ROMANCE
1017—THE SHERIFF*
1021—THE JUDGE*
1025—THE COP*

SILHOUETTE DESIRE
1035—IN ROARED FLINT
1071—ONE TICKET TO TEXAS
1229—PLAIN JANE'S TEXAN
1425—WILD ABOUT A TEXAN
1432—HER TEXAS TYCOON

*Texas Outlaws

For the members of Austin RWA and
my fabulous editor, Kathleen Scheibling

With special thanks to the Pattersons for
their help, and to Kit Frazier, who saved
my bacon, I dedicate a special sugar dance.

Chapter One

Exhausted from battling the blowing snow of a late winter storm, Belle Outlaw knew that she couldn't make it another mile. The skies had been clear when she left Colorado, but the weather had turned nasty. She'd hoped to make it to Texas but was now desperate to find a place to stop for the rest of the night. When she spotted a flickering motel sign ahead, she knew her prayers had been answered. Pulling the U-Haul trailer into the portico by the office, she stumbled out of her SUV and rented a room from the sleepy desk clerk.

"Bad out tonight," he said as he handed her the key to unit ten.

She only nodded.

Somehow Belle managed to drive to a place near the door of her assigned room, lock her SUV and make it inside. She didn't even try to bring in her overnight bag. It was well below freezing outside, but she was burning up. Fever, she knew. With her luck she'd probably die alone in some ratty motel room in the middle of nowhere, and the maid would find her when she came to clean the room.

She ought to call somebody—but who? She didn't want her

parents to worry about her, and her older brothers had families and didn't need to come charging to her rescue. That left Sam, her baby brother. Sam Outlaw, the Texas Ranger. Texas Rangers could handle anything.

It took three tries before she managed to correctly dial Sam's number—and four rings before he answered.

"Oh, Sam. Thank God you're home."

"Belle? Is that you? Where the hell else would I be? Do you know what time it is?"

"I give up."

"It's one o'clock in the morning."

"Sorry, Sam. Sorry. I need help. Come get me."

"Belle, have you been drinking? Where are you?"

"Only coffee. I don't know. A motel somewhere in New Mexico, I think. Or maybe I made it to Texas. I tried."

"Where's Matt?"

"Matt who?"

"Matt, your husband."

"I have no husband," Belle said. "Come get me, Sam. I think I'm dying."

"Belle, hon—"

The phone went dead. She let it drop, fell back on the bed and wrapped the spread around her like swaddling.

"GABE, GABE, WAKE UP!"

Gabe Burrell opened one eye. Where was he? Oh, yeah, Sam's lake house. "It can't be time to get up yet, Sam. I just got to sleep."

"Listen, we'll have to cancel our fishing trip. I think my sister's sick and I have to get to her pronto."

"What's wrong?"

"Damned if I know. She was talking crazy. But if Belle asked for help it has to be bad."

Gabe threw back the covers and grabbed his pants. "I'll go with you."

"I was hoping you'd say that. I traced the number to a little motel in a place that's a grease spot on the map near Dalhart in the panhandle, but now the phones are out in that area. I think there's a municipal airport nearby."

"Make us some coffee while I check out the weather conditions to see what we can fly."

BELLE FOUGHT TO OPEN her eyes, but they didn't want to cooperate. Everything was bright and blinding white, and she felt as if she were floating. Was she in heaven?

Shielding her eyes from the dazzling brightness, she made out the silhouette of a man. His hair was spun gold and lit by a bright halo.

"Who—who are you?" she croaked. Her tongue was thick, and her mouth felt packed with cotton batting.

"I'm Gabe Burrell."

"Gabriel? I thought St. Peter was in charge here. Where's your horn?"

He chuckled. "My horn? I don't have a horn, darlin'. Sorry."

"Gotta have a horn."

"Years ago I had a saxophone but it's long gone."

"No sax. A trumpet. Blow, Gabriel, blow."

He chuckled again, and she was going to ask what was funny, but she was too tired.

When she opened her eyes again, the angel was gone and Sam was sitting beside her.

"Sam?"

"In the flesh."

"Aren't we in heaven anymore?"

"No, Ding-dong, we're in the hospital. You've been sick. Pneumonia. You've been pretty much out of it for three days. How are you feeling?"

"Like an elephant's sitting on my chest. *Three days?*"

"Yep. You've been a mighty sick little gal. If Gabe Burrell hadn't flown me here, we might have lost you."

"Gabriel flew you here?"

"Yes."

"I didn't know he could take passengers. Did he find his horn?"

"What horn? Belle, honey, you're talking a little crazy. Gabe doesn't have a horn that I know about. And he flew me here in a helicopter."

"I guess angels don't use their wings anymore. They've gone high tech."

Sam laughed. "What in the world are you talking about? Gabe's no angel. Trust me on that."

"Are you sure?" Belle asked, but before she heard Sam's answer, she slipped away once more.

Belle didn't see her brother again until she was sitting up having breakfast. Nurse Ratched—or her clone—had checked her IV, cranked up the bed and taken the cover off some vile-looking mush.

"Eat," Nurse Ratched had said before she sailed out of the room.

Belle sneered at the gray glop on her plate. "She's got to be kidding."

"Who?" Sam said.

"Nurse Ratched. The warden who was just in here."

"I thought her name was Vivian Johnson. What was she kidding about?"

"Eating this stuff."

"You must be feeling better," said a blond man who followed Sam into the room.

"As compared to what?"

The man chuckled. Belle recognized the sound. "Gabriel? I thought I dreamed you."

"Gabe, just plain Gabe. Would you rather have a hamburger?"

"No, but I'd kill for a nice, thick milk shake."

"What flavor?"

"Strawberry."

"I'll be right back," Gabe said.

After he left, Belle said, "Who's he?"

"An old friend of mine. He's my insurance agent and fishing buddy. Now that you're back from the dead, you want to tell me what's going on with you and Matt? Last I heard after you quit the FBI and married him last Christmas, the two of you had settled down on his ranch in Colorado and were happy as a pair of beetles in dung."

"We were—or at least I thought we were until he came in one day and announced that he'd been seeing his old girlfriend again."

Sam looked shocked. "His old girlfriend? *Matt?*"

"You aren't any more surprised than I was. They grew up

together and were high-school sweethearts. Seems she came back to town after her marriage soured, and she and Matt got together. The ink wasn't even dry on our marriage license when she cried on his shoulder and one thing led to another. Now they're in love, and she's pregnant."

"The son of a bitch!"

"My sentiments exactly," Belle said.

"He can't do that to my sister! I'm going to Colorado and whip that bastard's ass."

Belle rolled her eyes. "Simmer down. You're not going anywhere. If I meant so little to him then I'm glad to be rid of him. We've already filed for divorce, and it should be final in a couple of weeks, but I was too sick of Colorado to stick around any longer. And may warts grow on my nose and my ears fall off before I go calf-eyed over a man again."

Gabriel strolled in, grinning and bearing a tall plastic cup. "At your service, ma'am. You like one straw or two?"

"Just one. Thanks."

He peeled the paper off the straw, stuck it into the cup and handed her the milk shake. She sucked up pure ambrosia. "Thanks. This is heavenly."

He looked pleased with himself. Now that she had a chance to examine him more closely, Belle could see that Sam's friend was far from angelic. He was devilishly handsome and his grin was straight from Old Scratch himself. Good thing she'd sworn off men or she might have been totally captivated by Gabriel. Gabe. She had to remember that—just plain Gabe.

"Gabe," Belle said, "thanks for flying Sam here. I understand that I might not be around if you two hadn't shown up. I wasn't even sure where I was."

"Glad to do it. It was good that you stopped when you did. There was a nasty storm going on."

"I remember the storm," she said, "but not much else after that. Sam, when can I get out of this place?"

"You'll have to ask your doctor, but I wouldn't count on it being for a while yet. You're still on intravenous antibiotics."

"But I don't like being sick."

"Belle," Sam said, "don't whine. You're lucky to be alive."

She slurped her milk shake. "You didn't call Mom and Dad, did you, Sam?"

"No. Sick as you were when we got here, you roused enough to get a death grip on my shirt and make me promise that I wouldn't. I haven't called anybody. Want me to?"

"Lord, no. You know I can't stand hovering. Cole nearly went bonkers from all their attention when he was laid up. When I'm feeling better, I'll call and tell them about—you know, the other." She slurped on the straw again, but the cup was dry.

"Want another one of those?" Gabe asked.

"Want? Yes. Can I hold it? No. I think my stomach shrank. Thanks for this one. I think I'll go to sleep for a while."

"I LIKE YOUR SISTER," Gabe said as he and Sam walked down the hall.

"Me, too," Sam said. "She's one of a kind. Did I ever tell you that she was an FBI agent?"

Gabe nodded. "I think you told me when you explained about the Outlaw family's tradition of being named after famous outlaws and all being in law enforcement. You're Sam Bass Outlaw, and she's Belle Starr Outlaw. And you have brothers Jesse James and Frank James."

Sam nodded. "J.J. is the sheriff of Naconiche County, and Frank is a judge there."

"And isn't there another brother?"

"Cole Younger Outlaw. He was a homicide cop in Houston, but he teaches criminal justice these days. My brothers are all married now and have families."

"Didn't I remember that Belle was married, too?"

"She was," Sam said. "She's getting a divorce. The SOB she married turned out to be a louse."

Gabe shouldn't have been pleased about that, but for some reason, he was. Even ill and without the usual female paint, Belle Outlaw was a stunning woman. She was gutsy for sure, and she had a great sense of humor. Plus, he'd seen a side of her that he doubted she showed very often. Her vulnerability. She'd drawn out his protective streak and made him want to bundle her up and cradle her like a baby. In short, she fascinated him.

"How are we going to work getting your sister back to Texas?" Gabe asked. "And exactly where are we going to take her? Is she planning to stay with you?"

"Beats me," Sam said. "I've been thinking about that some myself. I know you have a business to run, and you can't hang around here forever. I suppose you can take off anytime now, and I'll drive her back to Austin."

"I'm not in any hurry. Matter of fact, didn't you tell me that you have to go to an important training session next week?"

Sam nodded. "In Virginia. Since I have to be gone, and I'm in the middle of moving, I'm going to try to talk Belle into going home to Naconiche."

"She doesn't want to go?"

"Nope. I suspect that partly she's concerned about my mother's tendency to hover, but mostly I think she doesn't want to talk about the mess with Matt."

"The husband?"

"The soon to be ex-husband."

"Maybe she could fly home with me and stay in Wimberley to recuperate while you're gone. My sister will be there, and her clinic is right next to the house."

"Her clinic?" Sam asked. "What kind of clinic?"

"She a vet. And my mother is there, too. She's a little flaky, but she makes good chicken soup."

"Your mother or your sister?"

Gabe laughed. "My mother makes good chicken soup—when she remembers to put the chicken in the pot. She's an artist of sorts and a little flighty. She's not a hoverer for sure—more of a soarer, I'd say."

"Sounds…interesting."

Gabe grinned. "You don't know the half of it."

"I'm willing to park Belle with you if she's willing. I have to warn you though. Belle's as stubborn as a mule."

"So am I. Flora says it's my most endearing trait."

"Who's Flora?"

"My mother. I have a cook and a housekeeper if Flora forgets the chicken. Also, I think having someone her own age around will be good for my sister. Most of her friends are animals. We have a menagerie at our place. Belle's not allergic to animals, is she?"

"Lord, no. That's Cole, my oldest brother. And only to cats. We all grew up with lots of critters. Give Belle a horse or a dog, and she's happy as a pig in slop."

Gabe laughed. "Then she'll fit right in. Shall we go back and tell her our plans?"

Looking pained, Sam hesitated for a moment. "Let's wait and surprise her later."

Chapter Two

Belle wasn't exactly sure how it had happened. She blamed all the antibiotics for turning her brain to mush. But here she sat in a helicopter headed for Texas with a man she barely knew, albeit a very attractive man. And a kind one. She had to admit the flight in the chopper was less daunting than a road trip. Even so, she'd slept off and on for a good part of the time they'd spent in the air.

Rousing from her doze, she looked around, trying to get her bearings. "How much farther?" she asked Gabe. Because of the noise, they had to use headphones and mikes to talk.

"We'll be setting down in a few minutes. Are you tired?"

"Not so much tired as stiff. Are you sure that your family won't mind having a surprise houseguest?"

"They won't mind, and you're not a surprise. I called ahead so Suki could shoo the chickens and pigs out of the guest room."

Belle wasn't quite sure if he was teasing or not. She knew very little about Gabe except that he was Sam's friend and insurance agent. "Who's Suki?"

"The housekeeper."

"Is she Asian?"

"Some on her mother's side, I think. She's mostly a mixture like the rest of us. Suki's barely over five feet tall, but she's been ruling over the wild mob in our household for several years."

"You have a wild mob?"

"It seems that way sometimes. You'll soon have everybody straightened out."

Belle chewed on that for a while. Sounded like a zoo at his place, and what she needed was peace and quiet. Growing up with four brothers was like living with a wild mob, too, and she often retreated to her hidey-holes to escape the madness. While she adored her brothers and enjoyed people, she also enjoyed solitude. Since she'd left home for college, she'd lived alone, except for an occasional roommate, until she'd married Matt.

"You know, I don't think I've ever been to Wimberley. Exactly where is it in relation to Austin?"

"About forty or forty-five miles southwest. You were asleep when we buzzed the governor's mansion a few minutes ago. Didn't I hear Sam say that you'd gone to the University of Texas?"

"Only to law school. But except for occasional forays downtown to Sixth Street, I never ventured far from campus and my apartment. I pretty much kept my nose in my books."

"A high achiever, huh?"

Belle chuckled. "You've got my number. I've always been competitive. But with four brothers, what can you expect? Hustling was how I kept up."

Gabe smiled and turned his attention to piloting the chopper.

She saw a small town ahead, nestled among rolling hills and with a rocky river running through it. From her viewpoint, it looked like a picturesque village from a movie set.

"That's home," Gabe said, nodding toward a place at the edge of town.

She spotted their destination: a large stone house on a hill surrounded by a number of outbuildings. Horses grazed in a pasture, unfazed by the noise of the rotors, and she noticed several other animals as well, including what looked like a llama.

Gabe landed on a pad near a barnlike structure located a couple of hundred yards from the house. A Jeep Cherokee approached as they set down. And by the time the helicopter engine died, a burly man climbed from the vehicle and waved.

"That's Ralph," he told Belle. "Suki's husband, come to collect us."

Gabe hung up his earphones and climbed from the chopper. "How's it going, Ralph?"

"Can't complain. We had rain yesterday."

Gabe helped Belle from her seat. "Belle Outlaw, this is Ralph Sanderson."

Belle offered her hand. "Mr. Sanderson."

"Just Ralph will do, Ms. Outlaw."

His callused hand took hers in a no-nonsense grip. He had a sweet smile and the bluest eyes she'd ever seen. She judged him to be in his late fifties, maybe a bit younger.

"Just Belle will do, Ralph."

"Yes, ma'am."

Belle's legs wobbled a bit, and Gabe helped her to the Jeep's front passenger seat while Ralph got their luggage and stowed it in the back. In contrast to the snowstorm that felled her, Wimberley's weather was gorgeous: clear, sunny and mild.

She rolled the window down as Ralph drove them to the house, and caught a lovely scent. "What's that smell?"

"Good or bad?"

She smiled. "A sweet odor."

"You must mean the Texas mountain laurels," Gabe said. "They're in full bloom."

"Oh, yes, I remember now from when I lived in Austin. The little trees with the purple clusters. We don't have them in East Texas. I always thought they smelled like grape Kool-Aid."

"Never thought about that," Ralph said, "but, you know, I think you're right. What part of East Texas are you from, Belle?"

"A little town named Naconiche, right smack in the middle of the piney woods."

Ralph nodded. "Been through there. Beautiful area. I grew up in Fredericksburg myself."

"Heard of it, but I've never been there," Belle said. "Gabe, I don't think I know where you grew up. In this area, was it?"

"Mostly. My first few years we lived all over the place, and when my mother and stepfather married, we settled here."

The Jeep pulled to a stop in front of the house, which loomed even larger up close. Built of native limestone, the two-story structure spread out like a fortress on the hill and was shaded by oak trees, which were huge by Central Texas standards but would be called merely scrubs by East Texans. And the Texas mountain laurels, with their purple clusters of flowers, lined a tall fence that meandered along the foot of the hill some distance away.

"You folks go on in," Ralph said. "I'll get the bags."

As Gabe helped Belle up the steps to a large veranda that ran half the length of the house, a blood-curdling scream came from inside. An older woman in tie-dyed purple garb came running from the house and threw herself at Gabe.

"Oh, Gabriel! Thank heavens you're home. Do something! Do something!"

"Good lord, Mother!" a younger blond woman said as she charged outside, a large German shepherd at her side and a tiny, yapping Yorkie dancing behind. "We have a guest."

"Calm down, everybody!" a third woman yelled. "I killed it with the broom!" This one, smaller and darker than the first two, hurried out still clutching the red-handled straw broom.

"Exactly what did you kill?" Gabe asked as he extricated himself from the screamer.

"A puny, little scorpion," the executioner said. "Wasn't even full grown."

"But you know how I hate those awful things, Gabriel. It was in my bathroom. Why, I almost stepped on it. And the awful creature reared up and was about to attack me. I do believe it hissed at me."

"Mother," the blonde said, "it wasn't going to attack, only defend. And scorpions don't hiss." The tall woman stuck out her hand to Belle. "Hi, I'm Skye Walker, Gabe's sister. Welcome to Bedlam."

Belle smiled at Skye and returned the firm handshake. Skye, who looked to be about Belle's age, was dressed in jeans, sneakers and a faded blue jersey that advertised dog food. Even though her fair hair was cut short and she wore very little makeup—maybe lip gloss—Skye was stunning.

"Belle," Gabe said, "this slightly hysterical woman is my mother, Flora Walker."

"Oh, my dear," Flora said, capturing both Belle's hands in hers, "we're so delighted to have you here while you recover. You have the most magnificent cheekbones. And I love your eyes. They're the exact color of storm clouds. You must let me paint you."

The woman with the broom cleared her throat loudly. "I'm Suki, Ralph's wife. Now, everybody stand back, and let's get the poor girl in off the porch. She looks a mite peaked to me. Ralph, take them bags to the guest quarters."

"Wait!" Flora stepped in front of Ralph. "Don't take them up yet. Have Manuel spray in there first."

"Manuel is over at the kennel," Skye said. "And he just sprayed two days ago."

"Then he didn't do a very good job. We have an infestation of scorpions."

"Mother, one baby scorpion isn't an infestation," Gabe said.

"Where there's one baby, there's another. Or more. Those little beasties are prolific breeders." Flora grabbed Belle's arm. "You must be very careful, dear. Don't put on your shoes without shaking them. They love to hide in shoes. I've lived here for over thirty years, and I'm still not used to them."

If Belle had been in better form—and less polite—she would have laughed at Flora's theatrics. "Thanks for the warning. But I'm familiar with scorpions—and worse… beasties. I'll be careful."

Gabe's mother repinned the long braid that had slipped from its coil atop her wispy tendrils of gray-blond hair. "Why are we standing here on the porch? Let's all come inside and get Belle settled. Gabe, dear, it's good to have you home." She tiptoed to kiss her tall son's cheek, then sailed inside, leading the way.

Gabe glanced at Belle, shrugged his shoulders and smiled.

"I'd like to tell you that things aren't always so chaotic around here," he whispered, "but I'd be lying."

"Gabriel, what terrible secrets are you whispering to our guest?" Flora asked. "Belle, would you like something to drink? The sun is over the yardarm as they say somewhere or the other. You know, I've never been exactly sure what a yardarm is. In any case, we can offer you coffee, tea, a soft drink or something stronger. But I suppose that you shouldn't be drinking alcohol since you've been ill, though I don't imagine that a bit of wine would hurt. We have some excellent local wines, you know. I'm fond of the white zinfandel myself. And we have all kinds of juice. Orange, apple, grape."

"Mother," Skye said, "you're dithering."

"Oh, sorry. I suppose I am." Flora touched Belle's arm. "I do that when I get excited. Most of the time I'm calm as a cucumber. Or is that cool? I meditate, you know. Keeps me centered and serene."

Rather than be irritated by Flora's dithering, Belle found herself fascinated—and a bit charmed. The woman seemed to radiate a joie de vivre that enveloped everything in her sphere.

"I like white zinfandel myself," Belle said.

"Wonderful." Flora clapped her hands. "A kindred spirit. Suki, do we have plenty of zinfandel?"

"I reckon so. There's a case in the basement. Maybe two."

"Oh, wonderful. Gabriel, you've had several phone calls from the office. Your secretary is fit to be tied."

"Martha is always fit to be tied," Skye said. "Belle, how about I show you to your room before the wine starts to flow? You might want to freshen up and rest a bit from the flight."

"That would be great, thanks."

The dogs accompanied them to the stairs. Skye scooped up the Yorkie. "This is Tiger. Rub his tummy, and he's yours forever. And this fellow is Gus." She stroked the shepherd's head. "He's my sidekick and is very protective of me."

Belle held out the back of her hand to the large dog. Gus sniffed, then looked up at Skye, who nodded before he licked Belle's hand. "German shepherds are like that. My family had one when I was a kid. Tripoli used to sleep at the foot of my bed, and he saved my bacon a couple of times."

"We also have a couple of cats around—and assorted other creatures from time to time. I hope you're not allergic to animals."

"Nope," Belle said. "Gabe already asked me. I grew up around all sorts of critters from bullfrogs to Brahma bulls."

Skye stopped at a door upstairs. "This is the guest room. If you need anything, just give a yell. Come down when you're ready."

BELLE'S ROOM TURNED OUT to be rooms—a suite with a sitting room, bedroom and bath. With its soft gold-washed walls and hardwood floors, the suite, like the rest of the house she'd seen so far, looked as if a decorator had done it. The furnishings, done in creams, golds, soft blues and persimmon, were an eclectic mix of country French and contemporary with a few rustic pieces thrown in for interest. The result was quite beautiful. And expensive, she guessed. The Persian rugs looked like the real deal, and the artwork on the walls, from prints to paintings, was all signed.

Even so, the cream-colored couch looked cushy and comfortable and the king-size bed positively sumptuous and inviting. Nothing said, Don't sit on me or put your feet on the furniture.

And the bathroom was to die for. Done in stonelike tile and accented in the same colors as the rest of the suite, it had a glass-enclosed shower and a bathtub with jets. A real tub. She'd had nothing but sponge baths and showers for ages. Her sore muscles and aching bones would love this.

Before she did anything else, she started the water running in the tub and added a bit of lavender scent she found on the ledge. By the time she'd located a change of clothes and her shampoo, the tub had filled. She stripped and climbed in.

Ah, heaven. She could get used to this.

A LOUD BANGING on the door roused Belle.

"You okay in there?" a woman yelled.

It sounded like Suki. Belle noticed that the jets were still running, but the water had grown cool.

"I'm fine," she called. "Thanks. Just a minute." She punched off the jets, climbed from the tub and wrapped a persimmon-colored bathsheet around her before she opened the door.

"Sorry to disturb you," Suki said, "but we was worried about you, you being sick and all."

"No problem. I couldn't resist that tub, and I fell asleep."

"Supper's in an hour. You want me to bring a tray up to you?"

"Oh, no. I'll dress and be right down."

"We don't fancy up for meals around here except on special occasions. Just put on whatever you're comfortable in and come on down. We'll eat on the sunporch at the back of the house. You like tamales?"

"I *adore* tamales."

"Good. That's what we're having. Maria makes some of the best ones in these parts, and she knows how Gabe loves them. Course Skye's a vegetarian, and Miz Flora is almost one—she only eats chicken and fish—so they'll be having something else. I don't guess you're a vegetarian?"

"Nope. I like steak too much."

Suki laughed. "Me, too. And pork chops. And did you ever try to eat chili without any meat in it?"

"Not lately."

"Let me tell you, it's not the same with that tofu stuff. Maria—she does most of the cooking—can do wonders with just about anything, but even she can't perform miracles. You need any help getting dressed?"

"No, I'm fine," Belle said. "I'll be down in a shake."

Suki left and Belle finished drying off and dressed in khakis, loafers and a blue cotton sweater. A shampoo would have to wait. She brushed her hair, wound it and clipped it up, then slapped on a bit of makeup. In ten minutes, she was on her way downstairs.

She followed the sound of voices from the back of the house to a large den with big leather couches and the same eclectic mix of furniture. A fire was burning in the oversized stone fireplace—more for the ambience, Belle suspected, than for warmth.

Gabe, sipping from a drink, stood with his back to the fire. Skye, perched on a couch arm, had a wineglass, as did Flora, who was relaxing in a wing-backed chair. Gus lay at Skye's feet, Tiger and a cat lay napping together by the fire, and another cat dozed in Flora's lap.

Gabe noticed her first and smiled. "Feeling better?"

"Absolutely. Sorry I conked out. I couldn't believe I went to sleep when I slept most of the way here."

"Don't apologize," Skye said. "It's perfectly natural. Your body is still recovering, and sleep is a great healer."

"You just make yourself at home, dear, and think of us as family," Flora said. "Would you like a glass of wine?"

"I'd love one."

"Gabe?" Flora said.

"Zinfandel?" he asked Belle.

She nodded and went to stand near the space that Gabe left. When he returned with her glass, she said, "I love the fire."

"Me, too," Gabe said. "We won't be able to enjoy it much longer, but while the nights are still cool, we're using the last of the firewood."

"Ha!" Skye said. "Don't let him kid you. My brother's been known to light a fire and turn on the air-conditioning."

Gabe grinned. "Guilty."

"Belle," Flora said, "Gabe tells us that you're a spy. I don't think I've ever known a real spy. How very fascinating!"

Gabe shook his head. "I didn't say that she was a spy. I said that she was an FBI agent."

"Well, isn't that the same thing?"

"Not really," Belle said. "You might be thinking of the CIA."

"CIA, FBI, SPCA. I get all those initials mixed up." Flora held out her glass toward Gabe. "May I have just a tad more? Anyhow, I think it's exciting. What exactly does an agent do?"

Skye looked amused.

"A number of things that involve investigation of federal crimes," Belle said. "But I'm no longer an agent."

"Oh, that's a shame. What do you do now?"

"Nothing at the moment. All the people in my family are in law enforcement, but I'm not interested in pursuing the field anymore. I discovered I wasn't cut out for chasing bad guys. I want to explore other areas and find something that suits me better."

"Oh, wonderful," Flora said. "I adore new beginnings. They're so exciting. I've made several of them myself. Mostly with husbands. I've had three, you know."

"No," Belle said, "I didn't know."

"Yes, indeed. I'll tell you all about it some morning over coffee. Or while you're sitting for me."

"Sitting for you?"

"For your portrait."

Skye chuckled. "Mother paints everybody's portrait who'll sit still long enough. She's quite good."

"I do soul paintings," Flora said. "I find them very insightful."

"Soul paintings?"

"Don't ask," Gabe said.

"Now, children, don't make our guest nervous. Belle, is your room comfortable?"

"Very much so. It's beautifully decorated, as is the rest of the house."

"Lisa did it," Skye said. "Your suite was her last project before she flew the coop."

"Lisa?"

"Gabriel's former fiancée," Flora said. "She was a gifted decorator."

"And a real snot," Skye said.

Amused, Belle glanced at Gabe, who seemed to find the fire much more interesting than the pre-dinner conversation.

Chapter Three

Belle wanted to hear more about Lisa and her flying the coop, but she didn't ask and nobody volunteered any more on the subject. Just as well, she thought. She wasn't eager to discuss her failed love life, either.

They all ate together, along with Suki and Ralph, who seemed to be part of the family, at a long harvest table in the sunroom. Since it was well after dark when they dined, there wasn't a sun to see. Maria's tamales were indeed among the best Belle had ever eaten. Everything was delicious and when the meal was over, Suki and Skye cleared the table.

Everyone scattered to tend to various tasks, leaving Flora and Belle alone in the den.

"Let me show you around the house so you'll be familiar with everything," Flora said.

Belle followed her on a tour of the downstairs, through the formal living and dining rooms.

"Down that hall is Gabe's domain. He has his home office and private rooms there. And here is the library. We have quite a collection of popular fiction as well as classics. I like mysteries myself. And romance." Flora winked. "Help yourself to anything that suits your fancy."

"I will. I love to read," Belle said, selecting a couple of books that looked interesting.

"Upstairs Skye and I each have a suite, and I have my studio. Tomorrow, if you feel like it, I'd love to have you sit for me. You can read and I can sketch."

"You said something about soul paintings. Exactly what is that?"

"It's a bit hard to explain. It's probably best if you experience it. Anyhow, feel free to have the run of the place, but we do set the alarm system at night, so don't go wandering outside without the code. I never can remember what it is, but Gabe can explain all that later."

"Do Suki and Ralph live in?"

"Well, sort of. They have their own separate apartment over the garages. And Manuel and Maria have a place near the clinic. Other employees live off premises. Would you like some coffee or an after dinner drink?"

"No, thank you, Flora. If you don't mind, I think I'll go upstairs and read for a bit, then make an early night of it. I can't seem to get enough sleep."

BARKING ROUSED BELLE. Piercing screams made her shoot straight up. Bounding from her bed, she grabbed the Glock from her bag and ran to the hall.

She heard a noise behind her and swung around, both arms extended and ready to shoot.

"Whoa, whoa," Gabe said. "It's me."

Belle lowered the pistol. "Sorry. Old habits. I heard barking and screaming. Did your mother find another scorpion?"

He smiled and shook his head. "It was Skye this time. A nightmare, I think. I was just going to check on her." He went to Skye's door and unlocked it.

As Belle watched him, she realized that he was barefoot and wore only pajama bottoms, flannel ones in Black Watch plaid. His hair was rumpled from sleep. How in the world had he heard Skye all the way in his distant rooms? And why was Skye locked in her suite? Strange. Very strange.

He'd left the door open, and she was tempted to follow him inside. Instead she waited. She heard Gabe calming Gus and praising him. She also heard soft murmurs as if he were calming his sister as well. A few minutes later he came out, pulling the door shut behind him.

He seemed surprised to find Belle still there. And the rake of his eyes over her reminded her that she wore only a long T-shirt and socks. Her eyes did a little raking of their own. The man had a lovely chest and wonderful shoulders and an—

Gabe cleared his throat, and she quickly glanced up from his navel. What in the world was she doing staring at a man's navel and wondering about all sorts of things that could only get her into trouble?

"Is Skye okay?" Belle asked.

"She's fine. She has nightmares sometimes, especially when our routine is disturbed."

"Oh, is my being here causing the problem? Because if it is, I—"

"No, no. Not that at all. Something else entirely. In fact, I think your being here will be good for Skye. All she does is work, and she doesn't have many friends her own age. Say, I'd better let you get back to bed."

"No problem. With all the sleep I've had lately, I'm wide awake. I'll probably read some more of my mystery."

"Are you eager to return to it, or could I interest you in a cup of hot chocolate?"

"Hot chocolate sounds wonderful. Let me get a robe, and I'll meet you in the kitchen."

Besides slipping on a robe, Belle took long enough to run a brush through her hair and brush her teeth. Adding makeup would be a bit obvious, so she passed on that—though she was tempted to at least use a little lip gloss.

When she got to the kitchen, she noticed that Gabe had pulled on a T-shirt, but he hadn't brushed his hair.

"Is the instant kind okay?" he asked. "I've got milk in the microwave."

"Instant is fine. I don't think I've had the regular kind since I was about six. That's the year my mother started back teaching." Belle sat on a barstool at the granite-topped center island.

"I didn't realize your mother was a teacher. What did she teach?"

"She taught in elementary school. We teased her that it was BK, BK and AK. Before kids, between kids and after kids. She was a wonderful teacher."

Gabe poured the milk into two waiting mugs. "Want a marshmallow?"

"Sure."

He plunked one into each mug, then brought them to the island and sat on a stool next to her. "Does she still teach?"

"No, she retired and bought the Double Dip. It's an ice-cream shop on the square of Naconiche. Since my dad's retired as well, they turned our big house over to my brother Frank and his family, and they live in an apartment over the shop."

"Your father was a sheriff, wasn't he?"

"For years and years. Now my brother J.J. has the job. What about your father? I assume that, since you're Burrell, and Skye and your mom are Walkers, you have a different father."

Gabe sipped from his mug before he answered. "Right. He and my mom were flower children who traveled around here and there in a minivan. Typical of the times. I was only a toddler when he tripped on LSD and flew into the Grand Canyon. Needless to say, his flight had disastrous results."

"Oh, Gabe, I'm sorry."

"No need to be. I don't even remember him. He was from Wimberley, and I got his name and his inheritance. My mother and I lived in various communes that were popular at the time, and she met Charlie Walker, who was a brilliant potter. They married, left the commune life behind and moved to Wimberley. For a long time we lived in my grandparents' old house. It had stood vacant for a couple of years after my grandmother Burrell died."

"Did you ever meet your grandparents?"

"My father's folks? Once, I think. At my dad's funeral. He was their only son, and they didn't approve of his lifestyle. Or my mother's."

"So sad for them," Belle said, laying her hand over his. "They missed knowing you."

"True." He smiled and stroked her hand with two fingers, tracing the veins and leaving a tingling trail to the end of each nail and back up again.

Her other hand squeezed the mug in a death grip. His touch felt much too...sensuous. Much too good. She tried to break the tension by sipping from her drink, but the chocolate was gone.

"Want some more?" Gabe asked.

"More?"

"Hot chocolate."

She jerked her hand away, "No. No, thank you. We need to get to bed. I mean, *I* need to get to bed. You need to get to bed. It's two o'clock in the morning."

He chuckled and winked. "Gotcha. By the way, is it loaded?"

"What?"

"Your gun."

"Of course it's loaded."

"You're a handy lady to have around."

"I suppose that depends on your point of view," Belle said.

"From my point of view, it's excellent. I'm glad you're here. Shall I walk you to your room?"

She smiled. "I have a good sense of direction. I think I can find my way." She carried their mugs to the sink and rinsed them. "Good night."

THE HOT CHOCOLATE didn't calm Gabe. In fact, his time in the kitchen with Belle had revved him up. As he lay in bed and stared at the ceiling, every cell in his body stood on red alert.

Belle Outlaw was one hell of a woman. He'd never met anyone quite like her—certainly not while staring down the barrel of a gun. He'd known she was a former FBI agent, but he'd only seen her helpless and ill in the hospital. It hadn't sunk in that she was a formidable female. And gorgeous. His mother had seen the good bones immediately. He'd noticed the bones *and* the curves over them.

Gabe felt very comfortable with Belle, more so than with any woman in a long time. Even more so than with Lisa. But he dared not entertain the thought of any sort of serious relationship with Belle. He'd learned that lesson. Women expected more from him than he was able to commit. They weren't prepared to live with the entire family that he was responsible for. Lisa had made it abundantly clear that she intended for them to have a life and home separate from his mother and Skye, but that simply wasn't possible. He'd promised Charlie Walker, his stepfather, before he died that he would take care of the women. He meant to keep that promise to the best of his abilities. He'd fallen down on the job a couple of times with disastrous results and didn't intend to make the same mistakes again. Flora and Skye needed him. He was their rock, their protector, and if it meant sacrificing a life of his own with a demanding wife, then so be it.

In their last big fight before Lisa walked out of his life for good, she'd called him a sanctimonious martyr giving up his own happiness for two neurotic women. Still, not even for her could he shirk his responsibilities.

Of course there was the chance that Belle might not feel the same way. She didn't strike him as a high-maintenance type.

BELLE WAS WIDE AWAKE. The hot chocolate hadn't helped. Maybe the caffeine in the chocolate offset the calcium in the milk. She felt wired. And a bit foolish for charging to the rescue, gun in hand. She'd almost blown away her host. Not a good thing.

She already admired Gabe, and hearing the gentle manner in which he calmed his sister added points to his score. He was a genuinely nice man. Too bad she hadn't met him before she'd met Matt. But she hadn't. And no way was she going to consider a relationship with another man. In the first place she wasn't even divorced yet. In the second, she understood the dynamics of the rebound effect, and she refused to involve herself in such a situation. She wasn't the sort of woman who needed a man to complete her. She could take care of herself—or at least she'd be able to when she figured out what she was going to do careerwise. Getting her strength back and making some decisions about employment were her priorities. Complicating things with a man would be foolish. Even a guy as appealing as Gabe Burrell.

BELLE COULDN'T BELIEVE the time when she glanced at the clock the following morning. She never slept so late. Throwing back the covers, she was about to spring from the bed when she remembered that she didn't have anywhere to spring to. She didn't have a job to go to or chores to do. Instead of getting up, she stretched broadly and lolled around for another fifteen minutes before she rose and dressed in jeans and a light sweatshirt.

She followed her nose downstairs in search of coffee and found Suki in the kitchen.

"Good morning," Suki said. "How about some coffee?"

"I'd love some. I'm addicted to the stuff."

"Me, too. Go on in the sunroom. Flora's in there, and I'm rustling up some breakfast for her. I'll fix some for you as well. You fussy? Flora likes that cereal with nuts and berries and seeds she gets at the health food store."

"Sounds good to me," Belle said. "And I can help you fix it."

"Shoot, nothing to fix. Just scoop some in a bowl and pour some milk over it. You go on and sit down. Keep Flora company. Mugs and the coffeepot are on the table. Help yourself."

Flora smiled up at Belle when she slid into a seat at the table. "Good morning. Did you sleep well?"

Belle reached for the coffee. "Yes, thanks. I didn't mean to sleep so late. I'm usually up by six."

"Not me. I've never found sunrise all that exciting." Flora chuckled merrily. "I'm a night owl in a family of larks. Gabe has already left for the office, and Skye is at the clinic. Do you use cream? Or sweetener? Gabe drinks his coffee black, and Skye and I use only raw sugar or honey, but I think Suki keeps some of those little yellow packets around."

"Honey would be wonderful."

Flora moved the honey pot toward Belle. "This is local honey, the best kind. Only Suki uses cream in her coffee. I've tried to explain that it's not the best mixture, but—"

"But Suki is ornery and does as she pleases," Suki said as she brought in a tray. "I like cream in my coffee, and it hasn't given me a bellyache in all the years I've been drinking it." She placed bowls in front of Flora and Belle. "Now I tried this stuff once, and I had a bellyache that wouldn't quit."

"Suki has diverticulitis," Flora said. "She doesn't handle seeds well. I think it's the raspberries."

"You gonna tell her about my bunions, too?" Suki asked.

Belle stifled a laugh behind her mug.

"I'm sorry, Suki," Flora said. "That was indelicate of me."

Suki gave a curt nod. "We're about out of that cereal mix. Want me to pick some up today?"

"I can," Flora said. "I need to run by the gallery this afternoon and the health food shop is next door. Belle, if you feel up to it, you might like to go with me and see a bit of the town."

"She needs to sit on the porch and rest, not gallivant all over the countryside," Suki said.

"I don't intend to gallivant," Flora said, looking indignant. "There's not much to see of town anyway. Wimberley is very small, and we'll be in the car. We'll only walk a few steps into the gallery and a few steps next door to Daisy's. Daisy runs the health food store. She's an old friend."

"Thanks for your concern, but I'll be fine," Belle said to Suki, who looked as if she were about to argue. "I need a few things from the health food store myself."

"See that you take care," Suki said, "and don't overdo it. I'll get to my chores."

Suki left, and they finished their breakfast. Belle heard a vacuum cleaner somewhere in the house as she poured a second cup of coffee.

"Are you sure you don't mind sitting for me?" Flora asked. "I'm eager to make some preliminary sketches."

"No, I don't mind."

"Good." Flora hopped up. "Bring your coffee and let's sit on the front porch. The light's good there, and Suki will be happy you're getting some fresh air. I'll run upstairs and get my pencils and pad."

Belle found a sunny spot on the porch and sat in one of the large wooden rockers there. Her parents used to have rocking chairs on their front porch in Naconiche. Thinking of her folks made her feel a bit guilty. She really ought to let them know where she was and about the situation between Matt and her. It would be awkward if her mom called Matt's place looking for her. Belle had tried to head off that situation by calling home last week and casually mentioning that she would be involved in some out-of-town business and that she could be reached on her cell phone.

She promised herself that she'd call her parents the next day. Or the day after.

Odd that she felt more comfortable among strangers than her own family. It wasn't that her mother and father wouldn't understand—or her brothers and their wives. They would. They would gather her under their wings like a hen with chicks. And she'd have to admit that she'd failed. Belle hated failing. More than hated it. The word had been erased from her vocabulary. But in the past year, she'd failed as an FBI agent and failed as a wife.

Someone had once said that failure was character-building. Maybe so, but she didn't feel edified in any way. She felt like a first-class wuss, and to be sick and helpless on top of that had brought her to her knees. She didn't like the feeling. She didn't like it at all.

"You must be pondering weighty things," Flora said.

Belle relaxed the wrinkles she felt in her forehead. "Oh? How can you tell?"

"You have a very expressive face. And aura."

"Aura?"

Flora's lilting laugh blended in with the dewy scent of the mountain laurels. "Ah, you're such a skeptic on the surface and such a believer down deep. You've made the right decisions, and you'll find your way."

"Pardon?" Was Gabe's mother some sort of psychic?

Flora laughed again, sat down and began to sketch. "I'm not touched, you know. I simply have an ability to see my subjects more deeply than a camera sees them. I'm so glad Gabe brought you home with him. Skye always brings home lost puppies and stray cats. Gabe brings home people."

Belle wasn't quite sure how the take the comment. She didn't like to think of herself as the human version of a lost puppy. She'd always been tough and in control, goal-oriented. Now she felt rudderless. Maybe it was a good analogy.

"Oh, such lovely potential I see breaking through that facade," Flora said as she continued to sketch.

"Was Lisa a stray?" Oops. She hadn't meant to say that.

"No. Lisa was a shark."

"I've been called a shark a few times myself."

"Oh, no, dear," Flora said. "You're no shark. And no stray cat, either. You're an eagle. A young eagle almost ready to stretch her wings and fly. See?"

Flora turned her pad so that Belle could see it, and Belle gasped. The drawing, a quick pastel sketch, literally took her breath away. With only a few lines, the older woman had captured her likeness, but she'd also captured something more. If Belle looked at the paper a certain way, her features seemed to morph into those of an eagle soaring toward a brilliant multicolored sky.

"That's amazing," Belle said. "That's…that's…"

"The way you feel inside?"

"It's the way I want to feel inside. It's the way I used to feel when I was a child—just before I went to sleep."

"And you'll feel that way again. You've just taken a detour for a while."

"Are you psychic or something?" Belle asked, the word almost sticking in her throat. She'd never had much use for hocus-pocus stuff.

"Don't I wish. I'd do better at the lottery. Do you know that the most I've ever won is twenty-five dollars? And that was three years ago. Which reminds me, I need to pick up a ticket when we go out this afternoon."

Belle continued to rock in her chair, and Flora continued to sketch and draw out the story of her life. Belle told her all about growing up with four brothers in Naconiche, about her time in training for the FBI and, to her surprise, about her failed marriage. She couldn't believe that she was being such a blabbermouth, especially with a virtual stranger.

"It hurts terribly, doesn't it, dear? I found myself in the same situation with my last husband. I thought I knew him so well, and it turned out that I didn't know him at all."

"Skye's father?"

"Oh, no. Skye's father was a saint. I meant my third husband. He was a cad. Turn your head just a bit to the left. There. That's it."

"Well, hello, ladies," Gabe said from the steps.

Flora glanced up. "Oh, my. Is it lunchtime already?"

"Almost," Gabe said. "Has Mother had you posing all morning?"

"No, I slept most of the morning. We've only been out here—" Belle glanced at her watch. "I can't believe that we've been out here for three hours."

"Three hours!" Flora exclaimed. "It can't be."

Gabe leaned over and kissed his mother's cheek. "That's what you always say. You'll wear Belle out on her first day."

"Not likely," Belle said. "The time got away from me, too. I've been totally relaxed, rocking and talking."

"Have you spilled all your secrets to her yet?" Gabe asked. "Mother has that effect on people."

Belle chuckled. "Maybe it's good that you came home when you did. I might have blabbed classified information."

"Too late," Gabe said. "You told me everything you knew when you were in the hospital."

"You're kidding, right?"

"Nope. You were a regular chatterbox." When Belle scowled at him, Gabe threw up his hands and grinned. "I'm teasing. Don't shoot me."

"Gabriel, what a thing to say to our guest!"

Before either could respond, a Jeep roared up and pulled to a stop in front of the house. A door opened and the biggest, meanest-looking man Belle had ever seen climbed from behind the wheel.

Chapter Four

Belle had seen some tough customers in her day, but this guy topped the list. Figuring him to be in his late thirties and about six-nine or so, she'd guess his weight at around three hundred pounds. But he wasn't fat, just big. Huge. Think Shaq on steroids. He had arms and legs like tree trunks and shoulders wider than a bus grill. He wore jeans and a windbreaker with enough fabric to make a hang glider. His head was shaved, and a scar curved from the corner of one dark eye to the edge of his grim mouth. She grew very, very still, watching him.

Then the other door opened, and Skye got out, followed closely by Gus.

Gabe smiled at the man. "Hello, there, Napoleon. How's it going?"

"Fine, Mr. Burrell. Just fine. Good to have you back."

"Good to be back. Belle, this is Napoleon Jones, Skye's assistant."

The assistant nodded toward Belle. She nodded back.

Tiger came running from the house and practically leapt into Napoleon's arms. The big man laughed, a deep rich sound, and held the wiggling little dog gently against him as Tiger licked his face.

"How you doing, little guy," Napoleon said, scratching Tiger's head as the dog licked some more.

"Belle," Skye said, "I see that Mother already has you posing for her." Skye peeked over Flora's shoulder at the sketches. "Wow. That's really something, isn't it? Mother can see things that no one else does, but I think she's captured you beautifully."

"These are just quick sketches," Flora said. "The painting will be better. I'll start on it tomorrow. Shall we go in for lunch? I imagine that Maria has things ready."

Once inside at the table, Belle was shocked to see it laden with so much food. Enormous platters of meat and bowls of vegetables, along with salads and a tureen of soup, covered the huge table and sideboard. It looked more like a church potluck dinner than a simple lunch. She wondered about the waste since she and Skye and Flora had only soup and green salad.

She needn't have wondered. Napoleon packed it away like no one she'd ever seen—and with four brothers and their friends, she'd seen some world-class eaters in her day.

When Belle finished, she said to Flora, "If you'll excuse me, I'll go upstairs and freshen up for our errand."

"What errand?" Gabe asked.

"Your mother and I are driving into town."

"I need to stop by the gallery, and I need to pick up a few things from Daisy's," Flora said.

"Are you sure that you're up to the trip?" Gabe asked.

"I think so. If I get tired, I can wait in the car."

"I'll drive you," he said.

Flora winked at Belle. "That means he'll go along and supervise your activity level."

"I'm fully capable of supervising my own activity level." Belle's words came out a bit sharper than she'd intended, but she'd never taken to being monitored.

Skye snorted, then hid it behind a cough.

Gabe chuckled. "Of course you are. It's just that I've cleared my desk so that I have a couple of free hours, and I was hoping to take you for a drive around the village."

"That only takes five minutes," Skye said.

"True," Gabe said. "We'll circle the square twice."

"Don't forget that cereal," Suki said. "And it wouldn't hurt to pick up another quart of honey."

Napoleon didn't say a word. He merely ate. Ralph had kept pace with him for a few minutes, but he'd soon dropped out of the race.

GABE LOADED two paper-wrapped paintings into the back of his Lexus. He and Flora tried to insist that Belle ride up front with him, but she declined and climbed into the backseat instead, leaving a frustrated Flora to settle for the passenger seat.

Belle had a sneaking feeling that Flora was eager to play matchmaker. It wouldn't work. She wasn't interested in being matched with anyone—not even gorgeous Gabe.

They drove down the hill's long, curving road until they came to a gatehouse. Belle was surprised to see that it was manned by a guard.

Gabe smiled and nodded. "Roscoe."

Roscoe, a burly guy who looked like an ex-Marine, nodded back, then peered inside the car before he punched the gate open.

As they drove through, Belle said, "I'm surprised to see a guard on duty."

"We get a lot of folks who don't realize that ours is a private road," Gabe said. "And don't try to hop the fence. It's electrified to keep our critters in and others out."

"Electrified?" Belle said. "That seems a bit excessive."

He chuckled. "You don't know the deer around here. They can be very determined, and Suki has a fit if they get in her pea patch and herb garden."

"Suki grows wonderful herbs," Flora said. "And she'll be planting her garden soon. Nobody grows vegetables like Suki. Of course Ralph helps her with the heavy work, tilling and such."

"With all the limestone, I thought it might be too rocky around here for vegetable gardens," Belle said.

"It takes some doing, but there are areas where the soil has been enriched," Gabe said. "We even have a couple of vineyards around."

"Gabriel is a partner in one of them, aren't you, dear?" Flora said.

Belle allowed herself to be drawn into a conversation about local crops and wine, but she still thought it was odd to have an electrified fence and a guard at the gate. But then, she'd never lived on what could only be called an estate. In East Texas where she'd grown up, cattle guards and barbed wire served the purpose.

"This is Ranch Road Twelve," Gabe said. "If you go west and hang a right at Dripping Springs, you'll get to Austin.

This way takes us through Wimberley. Keep going and you'll reach San Marcos. From there you can go north to Austin or south to San Antonio."

"That's our only major grocery store," Flora said, pointing to a large building on a rise. "And there's the visitor's center."

"And this is Cypress Creek," Gabe said as they crossed a bridge that spanned a picturesque stream tumbling over a rocky ledge in a rush through town. "It joins the Blanco River just south of here."

"Blanco," Belle said. "I remember going to Blanco on a field trip when I was in junior high. Aren't there some dinosaur tracks there?"

"Yep," Gabe said, smiling. "In the next county. And this is the square. Except that it isn't exactly square." He pulled to a stop in front of a row of shops with wooden storefronts.

Belle glanced around at the colorful array of buildings. "Where's the courthouse?"

"In San Marcos."

"Pardon?"

"The courthouse for Hayes County is in San Marcos, the county seat," Gabe said.

"When you said 'square,' I assumed that you meant courthouse square. Like our square in Naconiche."

"No courthouse here," Gabe said. "We don't even have a jail."

"What do you do with the bad guys?" Belle asked.

Gabe smiled. "We don't have many bad guys, but the few assorted lawbreakers get carted off to the calaboose in San Marcos."

"No police force?"

"Nope," he said. "The county sheriff and his deputies handle things pretty well."

"We frown on crime," Flora said. "This is the Firefly, the gallery that handles my work." She pointed to a shop painted a sun-weathered blue. "And Daisy's Health Food is just beyond it."

Gabe retrieved the paintings from the trunk while Belle and Flora got out and went inside the gallery.

When the bell over the door jingled, a tall, slender man, with more hair on his chin than on his head, turned from his customers. His face brightened. "Flora! Dear heart. Your timing is perfect." He rushed over to envelop Flora in a hug, trailing a scent that reminded Belle of sweet potato pie and mint tea. "Where on earth have you been, darlin'? And who is this gorgeous lady with you?"

"This gorgeous lady is Belle Outlaw, our houseguest. Belle, this is Mason Perdue, the owner of the Firefly."

"Mr. Perdue." Belle offered her hand.

He grasped her hand in both of his and bowed slightly. "Mason will do. My late *fahtha* was Mr. Perdue. Are you an artist, Belle?"

"I'm afraid not."

The bell jingled again, and Gabe came inside carrying the two paintings. "Where shall I put these, Mason?"

"By my desk for now if you don't mind, Gabe. Belle, may I steal Flora away for a moment? These very nice people from San Antonio have stopped by and are absolutely enamored by her portraits. They'd like to discuss a commission with her."

"Mason," Flora whispered, "I wish you wouldn't put me on the spot like this. You know how I feel about it."

"Double your price, darlin'," Mason whispered back. "They're loaded, and I need to pay my light bill. Things have been slow this month."

Flora rolled her eyes and shrugged. "Excuse me, Belle."

"No problem. I'll look around."

"I'll give you the guided tour," Gabe said.

Amused, Belle asked, "Think I might get lost?" The gallery was no more than twenty feet square.

Gabe grinned. "You might lose yourself among all these bluebonnets."

Belle soon discovered what he meant. About half the paintings were landscapes, and most of those were of fields of wildflowers, primarily bluebonnets. But these weren't poor attempts by somebody's grandmother or a weekend hobbyist. They were beautifully done by a variety of artists.

"Are these local artists?" she asked.

"Most of them, I think," Gabe said.

"Why so many bluebonnets?"

"Tourists, my dear," Mason said from behind them. "They gobble them up—even the bad ones at the place down the street. By the end of wildflower season, we won't have a one left. I've tried to get Flora to paint more bluebonnets, but, alas, one is all she'll do for now. This is hers." He hung one of the canvases Gabe had brought in an empty spot on her left.

Belle moved toward it and stopped dead still. It took her breath away.

"You can almost see the unicorns frolicking in the mists, can't you?" Mason asked.

Unicorns? No. But she could almost see fairies dancing in the flower fields. "It's…spectacular." And the price discreetly displayed on a card in the corner was spectacular, too. It was well beyond her means—especially now that she didn't have a job.

"I'll wager that it's gone by the weekend," Mason said. He sighed. "God, what I wouldn't give to be able to paint like that."

"You don't paint?" Belle asked.

"Compared to Flora, I merely dabble. I'm mediocre at best."

"But an excellent teacher," Gabe said.

Mason sighed. "You know what they say. Those who can, do. Those who can't, teach."

"Oh, I don't know about that," Belle said. "My oldest brother was an outstanding cop, and now he's an excellent criminal justice teacher. I suspect that you're a very good artist."

"Good, I suppose, but not great. Look at these portraits of Flora's."

They walked along the display beside Flora's landscape, and Belle stopped again to draw a deep breath. Spectacular didn't begin to describe the three large paintings displayed there. A surreal quality radiated from the canvases, captivating her. Besides her own few pitiful attempts at sketching and watercolor, Belle didn't know a great deal about art, but she recognized brilliance.

These were brilliant.

Beyond brilliant.

The first was of Napoleon, Skye's assistant. His features were carved into a huge oak tree and into the craggy mountain behind it. Strength and endurance fairly shouted from the powerful painting, yet doves and a lamb rested among the tree branches and flowers grew at its base. Seeing the painting, Belle's feelings about Napoleon subtly shifted. Rather than thinking of him as mean-looking, she saw him as powerful and fierce, but gentle and protective at the same time.

The second portrait was Mason and, while it was very different, it was no less awesome. On canvas, Mason became a wizard with a display of colored light circles illuminating the background. Each circle contained a different symbol, some Belle recognized, some she didn't. A pied-piper sprightliness seemed to draw her to the twinkle in his eyes.

"Did she capture you?" Belle asked Mason.

"Absolutely. I'm astounded every time I look at it. Something stirs deep inside me."

The third painting was of a little girl, a blond fairy clad in wispy drapes of moonbeams, lying prone beside a glade's misty pool and surrounded by every type of animal from tigers to bunnies. The creatures seemed enamored of the fairy child, whose finger trailed in the water and spread ripples over the still surface.

A feeling of familiarity tugged at her, but Belle couldn't name the subject. "Who?"

"Skye," Gabe said. "She was about four or five."

"No wonder she became a vet," Belle said. "Wow."

"Wow, indeed," Mason said.

Feeling both energized and a bit drained, Belle moved on to look at the other paintings. None compared to Flora's.

By the time they'd completed the perimeter, Flora had finished with her conversation, and they went next door to the health food store.

"Are you feeling tired?" Gabe asked.

"Not at all," Belle said.

Flora introduced Belle to Daisy, the owner of the health food store. Daisy's name suited her perfectly. A short, no-nonsense person, the owner was a trifle plump with an open, smiling face and a headful of white ringlets. While Flora bought cereal and honey, Belle looked among the shelves for a few things.

"What are you looking for?" Gabe asked.

"Something to replace all the good stuff killed off by the antibiotics that I took in the hospital. And I need to detoxify."

"Sounds painful."

Belle laughed. "Not really."

Daisy joined them, offering help. When Belle related her needs, Daisy said, "I know just the thing." She grabbed a couple of bottles from the shelf, bustled to a rounder of pamphlets and pulled several. "These tell you everything you need to know. And I'd suggest some of our yogurt as well. It's made just down the road, and it's excellent. Delivered this morning." She retrieved two containers from the cooler. "Are you going to be with us long?"

"I hope not," Belle said.

Daisy and Flora both lifted eyebrows.

"Is that a reflection of our hospitality?" Gabe said, clearly amused.

"Oh, no. That came out wrong. The hospitality is first-rate, but I'm only here to get back on my feet after an illness. I'm hoping I'll be stronger in a few days."

"Or a few weeks," Gabe said.

"Wimberley has a special healing power," Daisy said.

"You'll be back up to snuff in no time. Why, just look at me. When I came here, the doctors said I had less than a year to live."

"I'm so sorry," Belle said.

"Don't be," Daisy replied with a grin. "That was fourteen years ago. I'm fit as a fiddle—except for my middle." She laughed at her own joke and rang up their purchases. "The ice-cream shop next door is my downfall."

"My mother owns an ice-cream shop in my home town," Belle told her. "I love the stuff, too. Banana nut sends me into ecstasy."

"I'll have to remember that," Gabe murmured beside her ear.

A sudden flush warmed her, and Belle glanced quickly at Flora and Daisy, but they hadn't heard. "Down, boy."

Gabe laughed. "Yes, ma'am. And for the record, chocolate does it for me. Want to stop in for a scoop? Or two?"

"Not today. I'm fading fast."

"Damn! Sorry I didn't pick up on that," he said, scowling. "Let me get you to the car."

From his fierce expression, Belle was afraid that he'd throw her over his shoulder and take off. "Take it easy, Gabe. I'm okay. Just getting a bit tired. I've gotten too used to my afternoon nap."

"You're pale as a ghost. I've let you do too much too soon."

"I'm fine, Gabe. Honestly."

He ignored her protests, grabbed the bags of merchandise and steered her out the door, leaving his mother to trail after them. He refused to listen to her objections and installed her in the front seat and began buckling her seat belt.

She slapped his hands. "I can do that!"

"Feeling out of sorts, are we?"

She bit back a snotty reply. She felt six years old again, and she didn't like it.

Belle had thought her brothers overly protective, but Gabe could hold his own with any of them. Her brothers' overbearing behavior had always rankled, but after years of hissing and spitting on her part, they'd finally learned to back off and keep their mouths shut. Most of the time. She hated coddling. She was tougher than a two-dollar steak, and she didn't need to be carried around on a silk pillow. The sooner Gabe Burrell figured that out, the better things would be.

Chapter Five

He'd done it again, Gabe thought. Belle couldn't have made it any plainer that he'd scored high on her irritation factor. "Sorry," he said. "I promised Sam that I'd look out for you, and I don't want that guy on my case."

"Better him than me. I'm twice as mean as Sam on his worst day."

He laughed. "I can't believe that."

She smiled, and his heart did a little flip. "Believe it. I really do appreciate your concern and your attentiveness, Gabe, but I don't respond well to mollycoddling."

"I'll try to remember that, but I'm a natural born mollycoddler. Be patient with me, Miss Belle." He tried his best to look pitiful.

She didn't look as if she bought his act. She rolled her eyes and snorted in the same way his sister did when he tried to talk his way around her.

"Want some ice cream?" he asked, nodding toward the shop down the way.

"Don't tempt me. I'll wait until another day."

"Maybe we can stop by after your doctor's appointment tomorrow."

"What doctor's appointment?"

"Oh, I forgot to mention that I called this morning and got an appointment for you."

Her eyebrow lifted. "Oh, really?"

"Now, don't go getting in an uproar again, Miss Belle. The hospital faxed information to a doctor here as terms of your dismissal. You're supposed to see her until you're fully recovered. Kaye Hamilton is my sister's internist, and I thought you might like her. We don't have a big selection in town, but we have some excellent doctors practicing here. I thought it would be easier than trying to drive to Austin or San Marcos. Okay?"

"Sure. I don't want to be difficult."

"Be difficult if you like," Flora said as she climbed in the car and caught the tail end of the conversation. "I love being difficult."

"Artists are allowed," Belle said. "Flora, you're a genius. I didn't realize how truly gifted you are. I'm impressed with your work."

Flora beamed. "Why, thank you, my dear."

"As much as I tried to convince myself otherwise, I simply wasn't cut out for law enforcement. After all those years of preparation, I hated my job, hated the politics and dreaded going to work. Maybe I'm simply the rebel of the family, but I've always wanted to do something creative like paint or sculpt or write."

"Then do it," Flora said.

"I wouldn't know how to begin."

"How did you learn to read and write?"

"I went to school."

"You can learn the basics of painting or sculpting or writing the same way. There are dozens of teachers around here. Why, I could probably give you a lesson when we get home."

"After her nap," Gabe said.

Belle shot him a sharp look, and he pulled an imaginary zipper across his mouth. She laughed, and he winked at her before he backed out and headed home.

ALTHOUGH IT PAINED HER to admit it, Belle really did need a nap. She'd planned to rest for a half hour or so, but when she awoke, it was almost time for dinner.

Going downstairs a few minutes later, she found the family assembled in the den.

"I'm so sorry to be such a sleepyhead," Belle said. "I simply died."

"You're supposed to be resting and recuperating," Gabe said. "No need for an apology."

"But I missed my art lesson."

Flora dismissed the concern with a flutter of her hand. "There'll be plenty of time for lessons. Would you like some wine?"

"I'd better stick with juice, or I may nod off in the mashed potatoes."

Skye chuckled as she poured a glass of apple juice from a carafe on the bar. "How did you enjoy the nickel tour of our fair city?"

Belle sipped from the glass Skye handed her. "I didn't get to see that much of it. I ran out of steam first, but I look forward to exploring all the shops and galleries. It's a very picturesque little town."

"We get a lot of tourists," Skye said, "and it has grown a bit in the past few years."

Suki soon called everyone to dinner, and after they ate, they watched a new Sandra Bullock DVD that Gabe had rented. When the movie was over, the group scattered, leaving only Belle and Gabe in the den.

"Is the house alarm set?" Belle asked.

"Yes, but I can turn it off. What do you need?"

"I just wanted to sit outside for a while and do some stargazing."

He picked up a throw from the sofa and held out his hand. "Come on. I need some stargazing myself."

She took the hand he offered. It was warm and strong.

Gabe punched numbers into a keypad near the front door, then led her outside to the front steps, past the overhang of the porch. The night air felt cool and crisp against her face, but pleasantly so.

"This way," he said, guiding her away from the house to an outcrop of large limestone boulders. He spread the throw over the tallest rock and helped her up. "I give you the Wimberley sky." He looked up and made a wide arc with his hand.

A pale half moon and millions of brilliant stars studded the sky. With no clouds to obscure the display, the result was breathtaking.

"It's beautiful," she said, stretching out on her back and gazing upward. "You know, Colorado is supposed to have the most fantastic skies, but, to me, nothing can compete with Texas."

"Yep." He was quiet for a moment, then started to sing, "The stars at night…"

She joined in with, "Are big and bright…"

They laughed and clapped and belted out a rousing chorus of "Deep in the Heart of Texas." They pieced together and sang another couple of verses, laughing and clapping louder as they went.

Belle was in the midst of a slightly naughty verse from her college days when a spotlight suddenly hit them. The words froze in her throat, and she bolted upright. A car door opened and, blinded by the light, she heard the unmistakable sound of a shotgun jacking a shell.

"Hold it, Dick," Gabe said, sitting up. "It's me."

The spotlight went off. "Oh, sorry, Mr. Burrell. From the noise, I thought coyotes must have gotten in."

Belle shoved her fist over her mouth to hold in the snort of laughter about to explode.

"Nope, we're singing."

"Oh. Sorry, sir. Real sorry I interrupted. I'll be getting along. Go right on with your singing. 'Night, sir. 'Night, ma'am."

Her eyes hadn't adjusted after the spotlight, so she couldn't see Dick, but she suspected that he was tugging on the brim of his hat and kicking himself in the butt.

"Good night, Dick," Gabe said.

"Good night, Dick," she echoed.

When the car drove away, she lay back and exploded into gales of laughter. Gabe lay back beside her, chuckling.

"Coyotes? *Coyotes?*" She laughed again.

"I didn't think we were that bad."

"Trust me. We were."

He rolled to his side and looked down at her. "I love to hear you laugh."

A little shiver stole over her. "You do?"

"Uh-huh. You cold?"

"Just a bit." She'd lied. Her shiver had nothing to do with being cold.

He drew the throw around her, tucking it between them and drawing her closer to him. "That better?"

"Not really," she said, thinking he'd move and they could go inside.

"Funny, but you feel warm to me." His mouth had moved very close to hers.

She meant to spout something snappy and sassy, but her brain shut down and her hormones started acting up.

Finally she managed to whisper, "This isn't a good idea."

"Are you sure?"

"Pretty sure."

Gabe sighed and rolled over to his back. "It felt like an excellent idea."

He was right, she thought as her gaze scanned the starry sky. It had felt like an excellent idea. But kissing him would have been a dumb move. Technically, she was still married, but that wasn't what stopped her. The marriage was over except for a formal piece of paper. Her emotions had taken a beating with Matt, and she wasn't ready to deal with any sort of romantic entanglement—not even a temporary one. Her heart felt battered and raw, although the laughter had helped.

She manufactured a big yawn.

"Tired?"

She nodded.

"We'd better go inside."

Belle sat up. "Thanks for inviting me to your observatory."

"Anytime." He stood and held out his hand to her.

It felt warm. And wonderful.

She sighed. The timing was lousy.

Inside, they said good night at the foot of the stairs.

"Want some hot chocolate?" Gabe asked.

Actually, that sounded good, but she said, "I think I'll pass tonight, but thanks." She went upstairs, and when she got to her door, she turned and looked toward the foyer. Gabe was standing there watching her. She gave a little flutter of her fingers and went inside.

DAMN, GABE THOUGHT, mentally kicking himself as he reset the alarm. He'd rushed her. What had happened to the patience that he prided himself on? Maybe their silliness had done it. He couldn't imagine Lisa sitting on a cold rock and singing at the top of her lungs. Off-key. She would have thought it juvenile. But then Lisa had been overly concerned with appearances and rather shallow, he realized.

His and Belle's shared laughter had done him a world of good. His step felt lighter as he made his rounds checking the house, and he found himself humming "Deep in the Heart of Texas" as he went to his home office to finish some paperwork.

Shadow, a smoky gray cat of unknown origin, lay curled in his chair.

"Sorry, fellow, but you're going to have to vacate." He picked up the cat and put him on the floor. "Where's your running buddy?"

Shadow merely meowed and looked grumpy at being disturbed. With a flick of his tail, he stalked to his second-favorite spot and jumped up onto a club chair in the corner.

PROPPED UP IN BED, Belle read the last few chapters of a really spooky Stephen King novel, then flicked off the light. The story would have given a lesser person the willies, but she was good at separating fact from fiction. She wasn't given to being fearful of things that went bump in the night—especially in this place. She'd gotten a look at the alarm system, and it was top-of-the-line.

Punching her pillow, Belle turned on her side and closed her eyes, but her brain was too active to sleep. A thousand thoughts flitted through her mind. Gabe and the near kiss. Guilt over not calling her family. She'd do that tomorrow. The sound of Gabe's laughter. That damned psychopathic character of King's. What was she going to do for a living? Where was she going to settle? What would Gabe's mouth have felt like? His body had felt too good as he stretched out next to—

Shaking away the mishmash in her head, Belle flopped on her back and went through a series of mental exercises to quiet her mind. Those exercises had been a godsend in highly charged times over the past few years.

Soon she could feel herself quiet and settle and drift into the first stage of sleep. A misty image of Gabe seemed to wait for her....

Something bumped her thighs, and Belle came alert. It moved slowly, stealthily over her belly and breasts. What? What moved?

When a damp, warm breath hit her face, her eyes flew open. She found herself staring into a pair of glowing eyes, and her heart almost stopped. Jumping from the bed, she went one way, and the creature yowled, skittered and went the other.

When she flicked on the lamp, a Siamese cat crouched on top of the chest. Her heart rate slowed, and she laughed. "Sorry, sweetie, but you startled me. Who are you?"

The cat didn't move. It stayed crouched, eyes darting, waiting.

Belle moved toward the Siamese, and it scrambled, sprang from the chest, and ran into the sitting room. She followed.

She couldn't see it anywhere. She peered under the couch, and two blue eyes peered back at her.

"Did you get trapped in here, kitty?" She scratched on the carpet and patted it.

The cat didn't move a whisker.

"Are you shy? I'll let you out." Belle went to the door of the suite and opened it wide. "Here, kitty, kitty."

The cat still didn't move.

"Okay, have it your way. I'm going to bed." She left the door ajar and went back into the bedroom.

Wide awake now, Belle tried her relaxation exercises again. They didn't work.

She was hungry. All she could think of was ice cream. Banana nut. Butter pecan. Strawberry. Chocolate. Pistachio. Even vanilla would do. Vanilla with hot fudge drizzled over it.

Was there any in the fridge downstairs?

She was a guest here. Guests didn't go rummaging around in the freezer in the middle of the night. She turned over.

Rocky road. Pralines and cream. Peach. Peppermint. Cookie dough. Chunky Monkey. Cherry Garcia. She'd even settle for orange sherbet.

Muttering accusations about her IQ, Belle threw back the covers, grabbed her robe and stole down the stairs. She hoped there weren't motion detectors in the kitchen or an alarm on the refrigerator.

Nothing started ringing, so she supposed she was safe. Night-lights lit her way, so she didn't turn on any overheads.

The freezer compartment of the fridge yielded only vegetables, ice, two bags of peaches, three bags of strawberries and toaster waffles. The waffles surprised her. She figured the family for a from-scratch-waffles type.

With the amount of cooking that went on in that household, there was bound to be a bigger freezer somewhere. She poked her head in the large pantry off the kitchen.

Bingo. Not one, but two humongous freezers. One held mostly meat and vegetables. The other held a variety of items.

Including ice cream. Three half gallons. Chocolate, butter pecan and strawberry. Suddenly, she couldn't decide, and her mouth watered at the anticipation of sweet, cold flavors on her tongue. Gathering all three cartons, she carried them back to the kitchen to find a bowl and a spoon—if she could wait long enough to put the ice cream in a bowl and scarf it up.

Bright lights suddenly blazed on, and she froze.

Gabe stood by the door, smiling. "Ah, an ice-cream thief. Unhand those cartons, lady."

"Gladly. They're co-o-old. But I'm not turning them over until I have a bowl of at least one of them. You try to stop me, and I really might have to shoot you." She plunked her loot on the island counter.

He grinned. "Having a snack attack?"

"Big-time."

"Me, too. I'll get the bowls and the spoons."

"Hurry, or I might have to start eating with my fingers or just smush my face into the carton."

He laughed. "Go for it if you can't hold yourself back."

"I'll bite the bullet. Got any chocolate sprinkles or pecans?" She started pulling the lids off the containers.

"I'll check the pantry." He set bowls, spoons and a scoop on the island and went to the pantry.

"Hurry. I can't wait much longer." She put a scoop of each variety in her bowl. "You want one of everything or just chocolate?"

"One of everything," he said as he returned with an armload. "I've got sprinkles, pecans, chocolate sauce, strawberry sauce and brandied pineapple." He plunked the items on the counter. "I think there's some of that whipped cream in a can somewhere." He went to the fridge and started rummaging around. He returned with a squirt can and a bottle of cherries. "Want to make it a banana split?" he asked, plucking a banana from the fruit bowl.

"Sure." With the chocolate sauce in one hand and the strawberry sauce in the other, she drizzled swirls over everything in her bowl while he peeled and split a banana.

A trail of chocolate covered the back of his hand as he laid two pieces of banana at the edges of her bowl.

"Oops, sorry."

"No problem." He licked the chocolate away, and she found herself watching the stroke of his tongue, mesmerized. "Say, aren't you supposed to put the chocolate sauce on the chocolate ice cream and the strawberry sauce on the strawberry and the pineapple on the other one?"

She glanced quickly down to her bowl. "Actually, that's not

exactly the way my mother does it, but I've never been a purist, and I don't like pineapple on ice cream. Like my brother Cole says, 'It's all going the same place anyhow, and as long as it tastes good, go for it.'"

She scattered sprinkles and pecans on top of her concoction, squirted a dollop of whipped cream over that and crowned it with two cherries. Picking up her spoon, she dived in while Gabe was still pouring chocolate sauce over the chocolate and strawberry sauce over the strawberry.

"Mmm." Belle closed her eyes and savored the cold stuff as it melted in her mouth and slid down her throat. "Now that's heaven."

"You've got whipped cream on your nose." Gabe touched the tip of her nose with his finger, then licked his finger.

Belle's spoon stopped midway to her mouth. His action seemed very...erotic. She fought one of those shivers she'd been prone to lately. But the shivers weren't from cold. They were from heat. Gabe was a very desirable man. Ignore the feeling, she told herself. She was *not* going to allow herself to even think about a man, especially a sexy blond hottie with eyes like—

"You're dripping."

"Pardon?"

"Your spoon is dripping." He handed her a napkin and smiled. "Feeling a little heat?"

"Heat? Me? Not at all. It's just a bit of brain freeze."

Chapter Six

She couldn't believe the dream she'd had, Belle thought as she roused. Very titillating and starring Gabe Burrell. It had been so real that she could still feel his warmth against her belly as she lay curled on her side.

The warmth felt very real. Too real.

Squinting against the light, she opened her eyes and looked down. Two bright blue eyes stared back at her. They weren't Gabe's. The Siamese had joined her sometime during the night.

"Good morning," she said to the cat. "I trust you slept well."

The cat roused and stretched, then crept closer to her face and touched its nose against hers.

"Are we friends now?"

The cat stepped on her face and rubbed its head against her hair, marking her, then switched its tail and leapt from the bed.

In a few seconds she heard a yowl from the sitting room. Then another.

Belle threw back the covers and climbed from her bed. "I'm coming, your majesty. I'm coming."

The Siamese sat by the door waiting and looking impatient.

She opened the hall door and let the cat out, then hurried to the bathroom to dress. She'd overslept again. Her late-night escapades were cutting into her usual routine.

"GOOD MORNING," Skye said, looking up from her newspaper. She sat at the dining table with a cup of coffee in front of her and Gus dozing at her feet.

"Good morning to you, too," Belle said. "Aren't you usually at the clinic by now?" She poured coffee for herself from the carafe.

"We're closed on Thursdays, so this is my day to goof off. Mother has already left for her club meeting, Gabe went to his office early, and Ralph and Suki are outside puttering with her garden. May I fix you some breakfast? I'm not as accomplished as Maria or Suki, but I can scramble an egg and manage the toaster. Most of the time." She grinned.

"You don't have to wait on me. I'll fix myself some cereal in a minute. I need caffeine first. Anything interesting in the paper?"

"Wars, floods and political yammering. This is the *Austin American-Statesman*. Want a section?"

"Sure. Whatever you've finished."

Skye handed over the front page section. "I've graduated to the comics. I save the best for last."

"I hear that." Belle glanced over the headlines while she dosed herself with caffeine. "Does Wimberley have a newspaper?"

"Yes, a small one. *The Wimberley Star.* But it only comes out twice a week—Wednesdays and Saturdays—and it's limited to local news and ads." Skye refilled her cup. "Gabe said to tell you that he'd be home at about a quarter of eleven to take you to the doctor. I think you'll like Dr. Hamilton. She's a sweetheart. I hope you don't mind if I tag along. Gabe and I usually have lunch out on Thursdays."

"I'm not interfering with your plans, am I?"

"Oh, heavens, no," Skye said. "I think it's just part of Gabe's tactics to get me out of the house. I tend to be a stay-at-home. Totally boring, I know. I'd better run upstairs and get dressed. Need any help ferreting out the cereal, or did your FBI training prepare you for that?"

Belle chuckled. "I can handle it. In fact, instead of cereal, I'm going to settle for a bowl of that yogurt we got at Daisy's yesterday."

"Great. See you later."

After Skye left, Belle went into the kitchen and dished up the yogurt. It was scrumptious. She poured a second cup of coffee and decided to take it out on the porch to drink.

The moment the front door swung open, an alarm cut loose with a raucous clanging, and she nearly jumped out of her skin. Coffee went everywhere, soaking her pants and sloshing on her shoes.

The noise would raise the dead, and she didn't have a clue as to how to shut the blasted thing off.

Ralph came running around the corner with Suki hot on his heels, wielding a hoe. A jeep screeched to a stop in front, and two men with twelve-gauge shotguns jumped from the vehicle.

"It was me," Belle said. "I'm sorry. I didn't realize that the alarm was on." She felt like a fool with everybody standing there gaping at her.

Ralph punched in a code, and the nerve-jangling noise

mercifully ceased. "It's all right, boys," he said to the two men. "False alarm."

"I'm really sorry, Ralph. It didn't occur to me that the alarm would be on during the day."

"No harm done, Miss Belle. Gabe should have warned you and given you the code."

"Look at you," Suki said. "You've ruined your clothes."

"And the floor," Belle said. "I'll go get paper towels."

"You'll do no such thing." Suki leaned her hoe against the wall. "I'll tend to it. You go upstairs and get out of those wet things, and I'll go see to Skye."

"I can let her know what happened when I go upstairs," Belle said.

"Best I do it. Did you burn yourself?"

"No, I'm fine. Just embarrassed."

"No need for that."

Suki hurried upstairs and Belle followed, meaning to apologize to Skye as well.

Suki stopped at Skye's door and said to Belle, "You go tend to that stain. Just leave your pants in the bathroom sink soaking in some cold water, and I'll see to them later."

"But I wanted to tell Skye—"

"You can tell her later. You're dripping on the rug."

Suki's harsh tone made Belle feel doubly stupid. "Sorry." She hurried to her room to change and soak her pants. She hadn't apologized so much since she'd spilled a bottle of ink on her mother's best tablecloth. And that had been twenty years ago.

Having an alarm set when you're alone, especially in the city, Belle could understand. But in places like Wimberley or Naconiche, during the day and with Ralph and Suki just outside, it seemed strange. Maybe it had just gotten set without someone thinking, as a matter of habit. Odd, but understandable.

After she cleaned up and changed, Belle went down the hall to speak with Skye. About to knock, she noticed the door was ajar, and heard Suki saying, "Are you sure you're all right, honey? You're still shaking like a wet dog. I can call Gabe."

"No need to call him. I'm fine, Suki. Don't fuss so. I just got a little claustrophobic in the safe room."

In the safe room? Good grief, were they expecting an invasion? Belle backed away quietly and went downstairs. She applauded people being security-conscious, but, from what she'd seen, this family bordered on excessive.

She noticed that her spill had been cleaned up, and Gabe was coming in the front door.

He smiled. "Good morning. Heard there was a bit of excitement around here."

"I was going out on the porch to have a cup of coffee, and I tripped the alarm and baptized the floor."

"My fault. I forgot to show you how the alarm works and give you the code. It's always on at night. During the day it's activated if only a couple of people are around, especially when one of them is Skye. She spooks easily."

"Oh?" She waited for more of an explanation, but he only nodded.

"Come here, and I'll explain how it works."

"I'm familiar with the system. I only need to know the code."

Gabe raised his eyebrows, then nodded. "Fourteen hundred and ninety-two."

"Columbus sailed the ocean blue."

He laughed. "You learned that, too?"

"I did. Did you?"

They both laughed. "I doubt that we'll ever be named poet laureate," he said, touching her shoulder. "If you'll excuse me, I'll run upstairs and check on Skye." He gave her shoulder a squeeze and hurried away.

Curiouser and curiouser.

Shrugging, she told herself that it wasn't any of her business and went to have that second cup of coffee she never got to drink.

SEVERAL PATIENTS were already waiting at the internist's outer office when the three of them arrived. Everyone seemed to know Gabe and Skye and spoke to them, and nobody raised an eyebrow at the German shepherd that accompanied them. Belle had been surprised when Gus came along, but it seemed that where Skye went, Gus went. The dog lay on the floor at Skye's feet.

"This is our houseguest, Belle Outlaw," Gabe said, introducing her to John Oates, the mayor, Sally Olds, owner of Head Lines Beauty Salon, and the Misses Alma and Thelma Culbertson, retired teachers, third and fourth grades, respectively. The elderly ladies looked like twins and dressed in identical outfits, except that Alma's was beige and Thelma's was navy. Or was it vice versa?

The nurse opened the door and called, "Miss Culbertson."

Both ladies rose and went in, navy trailing beige. The mayor moved into a seat the twins had vacated beside Skye and began talking to her about Commander, presumably a dog.

Belle had taken a seat next to Sally, an attractive redhead

in her thirties with a stylish haircut. She was good advertisement for her shop.

"I'm happy to meet you," Belle said, touching her hair. "I'm in desperate need of a trim."

Sally glanced up from the magazine in her lap. "You have beautiful hair. Call me, and I'll work you in next week." She took a card from her bag and handed it to Belle. "Where are you from?"

"Originally from East Texas, lately from Colorado, but I'm planning on relocating to Texas soon."

"I hope you'll relocate to Wimberley," the mayor said, smiling broadly. "We have a fine town here, and beautiful ladies are always welcome."

"Down, boy," Gabe said.

John, who was probably about Gabe's age, only laughed. "Trying to cut out the competition, huh?"

Their bantering was good-natured, which put Belle at ease. From the calf-eyed looks the mayor gave Skye, obviously he wasn't interested in anyone else. Skye didn't seem to return his interest. She was merely polite.

Discounting Lisa the shark, it seemed odd that both Gabe and his sister were single. She wondered why. Maybe the pickings were slim in Wimberley. They certainly were in Naconiche.

The mayor was called in first, then Sally. Two new patients arrived before Belle was ushered in at eleven thirty-five. Why was it that doctors were always behind schedule?

It turned out that she did like Dr. Kaye Hamilton, a warm, no-nonsense woman with what Belle suspected was prematurely gray hair. After the doctor listened to her chest and asked a few questions, she said that Belle seemed to be progressing nicely. "Continue the medications you have and take life easy for a while yet. I'd like to see you in two weeks for a follow-up, but I don't anticipate any problems."

Belle smiled as she exited the doctor's office.

"Good news?" Gabe asked as he and Skye joined her.

"She wants to see me again in a couple of weeks, but so far, so good."

THEY HAD LUNCH at a restaurant on the square, one that had both vegetarian and regular meals and didn't seem to mind that Gus came in with them. Skye selected a veggie casserole and Gabe ordered the chicken-fried steak special.

"You are *so* bad," Belle told him. "I rarely eat fried food, but do you know how long it's been since I had a decent chicken-fried steak?"

"They're really good here," Gabe said. "Go ahead. Live dangerously."

She changed her mind a dozen times, but when the waitress started looking impatient, Belle slapped her menu shut and said, "I'll have the chicken-fried steak and iced tea."

"Good for you," Gabe said.

"I figure my arteries can handle it just this once."

When their orders came, Belle was glad she'd listened to him. Her steak looked wonderful and tasted even better.

"I don't know much about your family, Belle," Skye said. "Tell us about them."

"Well, my dad is a retired sheriff, and my mom retired from teaching and bought the Double Dip, an ice-cream shop on the square in Naconiche. They decided that their big old house was too much for them, so they moved to town and live in an apartment over the shop. Frank, one of my bothers who was a widower, moved in to the house with his twins and housekeeper."

"Is he the one who's the judge?" Gabe asked.

"Yes. County court at law. He's remarried to a land man."

They both looked at her strangely.

Belle chuckled. "At least she was a land man. They met when she came to Naconiche to lease property for her oil company."

"Oh," Gabe said. "That kind of land man."

"Right. Carrie practices law in Naconiche now. My brother J.J. is the county sheriff, and he married his former sweetheart, Mary Beth, when she came back to town with her daughter and a broken leg and opened a tea room and a motel. Of course the motel, which she inherited, was a weed-infested mess that had been boarded up for years, and she was broke."

"That sounds like an interesting story," Skye said.

"Very. She and her daughter lived in a vacant Mexican restaurant until she, with the help of J.J. and some friends, converted it into a tea room. She's a wonderful cook and it's been very successful."

"They lived in a *restaurant*?"

Belle paused to take another bite of her lunch. "Yep. And then there's my brother Cole, a former homicide cop in Houston. After he was wounded on the job, he retired and moved back to Naconiche to teach criminal justice at the community college in a nearby town. He married the family doctor—Kelly Martin. They have an adorable baby daughter."

"And then there's Sam," Gabe said. "I'll tell her about Sam while you finish your lunch."

"Sam's the one you know, right?" Skye asked her brother.

"Right. He's a Texas Ranger, the youngest of the brothers,

and he's not married. He was engaged, I believe, but it didn't last long."

"It sounds as if the Outlaw family is really into law and order."

"Family tradition," Belle said, pushing her plate back. "My grandfather was a PR genius before his time. He encouraged his offspring to go into public service and figured that name recognition was a good thing, so all the Outlaws are named after famous outlaws. Cole Younger, Frank James, Jesse James, Sam Bass and me—Belle Starr. My dad was John Wesley Hardin Outlaw, better known at Wes."

"Oh, my heavens," Skye said. "How fascinating."

"Indeed," Belle said.

"Dessert anyone?" Gabe asked.

"You've got to be kidding," Belle said.

"They make a killer peach cobbler here," he said. "With ice cream."

"Want to share one?" Skye asked.

Belle hesitated for a moment. "Why not go for broke? Order three spoons."

Gabe told the waitress to divide a cobbler three ways, but when it came Belle couldn't see any sign of its being divided. Her portion was huge.

But she ate every bite. Killer cobbler was right. She felt as if she might explode. Why had she been such a pig? She needed to get back into some form of exercise—walking at least.

Gabe and Skye planned to fly to Austin in the helicopter. Skye had a meeting and Gabe had some business to tend to, so they dropped her off at the house on their way to the pad. She would have enjoyed flying with them, but Gabe wouldn't hear of it.

"We'll be gone most of the afternoon, and you need to rest."

Rest. She was getting sick of resting. But she had to admit that her energy was fading fast. Maybe Flora would give her an art lesson later.

AFTER HER USUAL SIESTA, Belle slipped on jeans and a T-shirt and went downstairs in search of coffee. She found Suki making a fresh pot.

"Ah, a woman after my heart," Belle said.

"I just made some banana bread if you want a snack to go with it."

"I'm still full from lunch, but I'd like some coffee."

"I'm taking some out to Flora as soon as it drips. Go on out on the porch with her, and I'll bring a tray directly."

Belle headed for the front door, making sure that the alarm was off before she opened it. She found Flora leaning on the railing, laughing.

"What's going on?" Belle asked.

"Carlotta got out, and Ralph is having a hard time catching her."

"Carlotta?"

"A llama who thinks she's a person. Every time she gets out of her pen, she tries to get into the house. She's even learned to ring the doorbell. Actually, I think Skye taught her to do that, but a few minutes ago Suki nearly had a coronary when she opened the front door, thinking we had a caller, and it was Carlotta. She almost pushed her way past Suki before she could get the door closed."

Belle watched Ralph trying to corral the llama. Carlotta had the upper hand. "Ralph looks like he could use some help."

"He'll manage," Suki said as she carried out a tray. "Eventually. I brought a banana. Carlotta loves bananas."

"I'll give him a hand," Belle said. She grabbed the banana off the tray and hurried out in Ralph's direction.

When she got close, she half peeled the banana and pinched a small piece off the end. As soon as Carlotta spied the treat, she came running.

"Hello, girl. Want some of this?" She held out her hand.

Carlotta watched Belle for a moment with her big beautiful eyes, then slowly approached to nibble from Belle's hand.

Belle patted her and gave her another small piece.

Ralph ran up, winded. "She's a slick one when she doesn't want to be caught. She likes you."

Belle laughed. "I think she likes the banana better." She fed the llama a third piece while Ralph put a halter on her.

"I've got her now," he said. "Come on, you ornery animal. I'm gonna have to put a better lock on that gate."

Carlotta balked.

"Hey, sweet pea," Belle said softly, grabbing the other side of the halter. "Calm down, darlin'."

Carlotta stopped, eyeing the banana.

"One more piece if you'll go back to the pasture." Belle started walking toward the gate, and the llama followed, nudging her shoulder.

Once through the gate, Belle gave Carlotta another piece, another pat, then went out and closed the gate behind her. "Good girl."

"You've got a way with animals," Ralph said.

"I grew up on a ranch but I've never met a llama before. She's very smart."

"And spoiled rotten. She's not good for anything except as a pet. She used to be in a petting zoo before she got too big, and Skye took her in. Hard to find a home for her."

"I think she's lonely."

"Likely. That's what Skye says. I look to see a herd of them any day now."

"Skye's a sucker, huh?"

Ralph nodded. "If it's got four legs, it can find a home here."

"What about the two-legged variety?"

"Only if they're birds."

Belle laughed.

"I'm going back to the house and have a cup of coffee. You comin'?"

"I think I'll stay and talk to Carlotta for a while." She handed him the rest of the banana. "I'll be there in a minute."

She climbed on the fence made of concrete boards that looked like wood and sat on the top rail. Carlotta joined her, nuzzling her hands, looking for another treat.

"Sorry, girl, all gone." She rubbed the llama's nose and head. "You're just a big old teddy bear. The one thing I'll miss about Matt is being around the animals. We had a ranch, you know. And I had a horse named Sunset. Broke my heart to leave Sunset."

Carlotta looked at Belle with big, sorrowful eyes and bobbled her head as if nodding.

"But I'll survive. Maybe one of these days I'll have a place where I can have another horse. Just as soon as I figure out what I'm going to be when I grow up. Know of any jobs for an ex-FBI agent?"

A helicopter flew over and Belle waved. "Must be Gabe and Skye home from Austin." Her spirits lifted a notch.

Chapter Seven

The Jeep stopped, and Gabe got out. Skye and Gus followed close behind.

"I see you've met Carlotta," Gabe said.

"She got out of the pasture, and Ralph had some trouble getting her back in, so I helped him. She's a sweetie pie."

Skye stepped up on the fence rail and stroked Carlotta, who almost went into spasms of joy. "Yes, she is. But she's lonely. I'm going to have to find her some playmates."

"Oh, great," Gabe said. "Just what we need—more animals."

"Don't fuss, brother dear. Who bought two new horses last month?"

He gave her a look of pure innocence. "Mother?"

Skye snorted. "Gus and I are going to walk back to the house. Coming?"

"In a minute," he said. "I'll watch you from here."

She hesitated a moment, then said, "I'll see you guys later."

Gabe leaned against the fence near Belle and watched as Skye walked to the house. He didn't take his eyes off her until she reached the porch where Flora, Suki and Ralph sat.

What was the big deal about a grown woman needing an

escort for a few dozen yards? She itched to know. Polite or not, her curiosity poked her into asking, "Does Skye have security issues?"

"Yes, she does."

"Did something happen to her?"

Gabe leaned against the fence and rested his forearms on the top rail. Looking off into the distance, he was quiet for a moment. "Yes, something quiet traumatic. I do everything I can to make her feel safe."

"I see." She waited for him to reveal more, but he didn't. And she didn't want to interrogate him, despite her natural inclination to do so. Not knowing, her imagination went wild. She could picture everything from rape to a murder attempt. Had she been shot? Stabbed? Stalked? What had happened to spook her so?

"Do you ride?" Gabe asked, climbing up to sit beside her while she patted Carlotta.

"Pardon?"

"Do you ride? Horses?"

"Oh," Belle said. "Yes, of course. I've ridden all my life. Before you got here, I was just thinking about— Oh, never mind."

"Tell me."

"I was just thinking about having to leave Sunset, my mare, in Colorado. I adored that horse."

Gabe rubbed her back in a comforting gesture. "Can you get her back?"

"Oh, I probably could if I made a fuss, but…well, it's complicated. And impractical, right now. It's best that I leave everything there except the stuff I brought on the trailer."

Feeling uncomfortable discussing her personal business, she said, "Oh, by the way, I talked to Sam earlier this afternoon. He has stored my things at his lake house, and he's rounding up things so he can leave this weekend for Virginia."

"Have you talked to your folks yet?"

Belle sighed. "I'm going to call them tonight."

His hand was still on her back, and he continued to stroke lazy circles there. The feeling had gone from comforting to…something else.

She should move; she really should.

But it felt too good.

Belle would have sat there until sunup, basking in his touch, if Gabe hadn't finally said, "I need to make some phone calls. Want to ride back with me or stay here a while?"

"I'll stay here a while."

Gabe climbed down and drove the Jeep toward the house.

She stroked Carlotta some more. "Feels good to have somebody's hands on you, doesn't it, girl?"

THE FOLLOWING MORNING after breakfast, Flora suggested giving Belle her first art lesson. "We'll do some sketching," Flora said. "Take your coffee out onto the porch, and I'll run up and get some supplies."

Excitement zinged through Belle. Strange that anticipating a simple art lesson revved her up so. Then, maybe it wasn't so strange. Even as a little girl, she used to dream of doing something creative—painting or sculpting or dancing or playing the piano or singing. All the time she played cops and robbers with her brothers, she secretly fantasized about being a ballerina in a tutu.

When she was about eight, she'd begged Mama for dance lessons, and, of course, her mother arranged it. They had bought pink tights and a leotard and little slippers with elastic. Belle could hardly wait for her first class. Even enduring her brothers' merciless teasing about her "girly stuff" wasn't enough to quash her exhilaration.

Things didn't quite work out the way they had in her imagination. Ballet was incredibly hard, and her feet and legs didn't seem to work just right. And if she managed to get her feet going, her arms and hands were off. "Gracefully, dear, gracefully," her teacher was always saying.

She'd sneaked off into the barn and practiced and practiced her positions, pliés, arabesques and glissades. Sam had teased her terribly until she'd jumped on him, pummeled him and bloodied his nose.

After a few months, the teacher very kindly told Belle's mother that, while she tried very hard, the poor child had two left feet, and that the Outlaws ought to save their money. Belle had accidentally overheard the conversation. She'd been crushed. That night she shoved her ballet slippers to the back of her closet and decided that she'd be a singer.

For a week she went around singing "America the Beautiful" and "Addicted to Love." Loudly and with feeling. Sam put cotton in his ears. Cole said, "Ding-dong, if you're gonna sing, at least sing on key." And her father finally yelled, "Stop that caterwauling!"

So much for her fantasy of being a chanteuse. She couldn't, as old man Hankins would say, carry a tune in a bucket. And her instrumental prowess was limited to playing the triangle in the second-grade band.

But she could run like the wind, so she played soccer instead. Her feet worked right on the soccer field. And she could yell, so she put her caterwauling to good use and became a cheerleader. She'd decided that, since she was a dud in the creative and performing arts, she'd have to rely on brains and brawn. While she was relegated to being an extra in high school plays, she became valedictorian and captain of the basketball team. She even learned to dance well enough to hold her own at the senior prom.

Still, every once in a while she imagined herself in a tutu.

Or in an artist's smock dabbing paint on a canvas.

Or in a garret writing poetry or the great American novel.

Or—

Belle stopped her musing when Flora appeared with sketchbooks and pencils.

"Today," Flora said, "I thought we'd start with perspective. Let's focus on that tree and the fence line."

Flora was the soul of patience as she pointed out things to be aware of and how to transfer what Belle saw onto the paper.

Belle worked for two hours trying to get it right. What she saw in the landscape wasn't what she drew on the paper. Somewhere between eye and hand a major block created big problems. With her gum eraser, she rubbed holes in the paper trying to sketch and resketch the tree and the fence. She was so wrapped up in her task, she didn't hear Gabe arrive.

"What are you doing there?" he asked.

Belle glanced up from her pad. "Sketching."

"Ahh," he said, looking over her shoulder. "Tell me about it."

She rolled her eyes. That was exactly the sort of thing she said to her five-year-old niece and nephew when she didn't have a clue what they'd drawn with their crayons.

"This is a climbing rosebush beside a porch railing."

"Of course," Gabe said. "Very nice."

Belle ripped the page from the sketchbook and crumpled it into a wad. "So much for my sketching ability."

"Why did you do that?" he asked. "It wasn't that bad."

She only rolled her eyes again.

"Dear," Flora said, "Belle and I were sketching that tree and the fence line."

"Oh. I'm sorry, Belle. I'm really sorry." He put his hand on her shoulder.

"Don't worry about it. When it comes to artistic criticism, I've developed a hide like an elephant."

"You mustn't be discouraged so quickly," Flora said. "I'm really not a very good teacher. Now Mason at the Firefly gallery is excellent. We can check and see if there are any new classes starting soon."

"Perhaps," Belle said. "If you'll excuse me, I'm going to run upstairs for a moment." She felt really stupid, but despite her best efforts, tears stung her eyes. She wanted to get away before they fell and embarrassed her and made everyone uncomfortable. She rose and hurried inside.

Gabe followed her. Inside. Up the stairs.

Fighting the urge to tell him to go away, she stepped up her pace. So did he.

"Belle, honest to God, I wouldn't hurt you for anything. I was born with one foot in my mouth. Ask my mother."

Stopping at her door, she said, "Forget it. Honestly, it's no big deal."

He grasped her shoulders and searched her eyes with his. Damn! He could probably see the tears. She glanced over his shoulder and struggled furiously to control them.

He suddenly hugged her to him. "It *is* a big deal. I'm so sorry."

Why did he have to be so blamed sweet about it? She could feel the tears coming despite all she could do. She sniffed.

Holding her away, Gabe studied her carefully. A stricken expression came over his face. "Oh, God, I've made you cry." He hugged her to him again. "Shhh."

"I feel like such a fool."

"You're not a fool. You're a normal person with feelings."

"I'm not a normal person. I'm an FBI agent. Was an FBI agent. I need to blow my nose."

He searched his pockets. "I don't have anything to offer except a gasoline receipt. Come on," he said, opening her door, "let's go get a tissue."

"I can handle it."

Ignoring her protests, he steered her into her bathroom and plucked a tissue from a holder on the counter. He held it to her nose. "Blow."

She blew.

He took another tissue and dabbed her eyes.

"I don't know what's the matter with me. Honestly, I never cry. I haven't cried in years."

"You've had a lot to cry about lately. You're entitled." He lifted her chin and kissed her lightly.

His lips lingered.

She didn't push him away.

His arms went around her, and the pressure from his mouth increased. She melted against him.

A knock at the door came, and they jumped apart.

"Lunch is ready," Suki called.

She must have looked as stunned as she felt, for Gabe said quickly, "I'm sorry. Forget that I did that." Turning, he walked away.

Forget it? She touched her lips. Not likely.

GABE COULD HAVE kicked himself. What had made him do such a stupid thing as kiss Belle?

Dumb question.

But still, it was stupid. He ought to have better control of himself. Sam had entrusted his sister to Gabe. He was supposed to take care of her, not take advantage of her. Belle was in a vulnerable situation and not even divorced from that louse she married. Right now she needed a friend, not a lover.

But he'd been attracted to her from the first moment he saw her, and his heart had about melted when she cried. All he'd meant to do was comfort her and make up for his gaff about her sketch.

But her lips had felt so damned sweet and her body so damned lush, that he'd let his instincts get away from him. Where would it have ended if Suki hadn't interrupted?

He smacked himself in the head. *Shape up, Burrell!*

Now he'd made things awkward between them. He needed to discuss the situation with Belle. But not now. The way he felt, he'd probably kiss her again.

He met his mother in the foyer, and she looked troubled.

"Is Belle all right?" Flora asked.

"I think so. She'll be down in a few minutes."

"The poor child doesn't have a speck of natural drawing ability," Flora whispered. "I don't know what to do. I don't want to hurt her feelings."

Gabe kissed his mother's cheek. "No, I did that pretty well. I think you should do with her what you did with me when you discovered that I hadn't inherited your talent."

"And what's that?"

"Encourage her in other artistic directions. There's always soap carving."

Flora laughed. "Don't remind me. For years I couldn't take a bath without using a misshapen duck or badger."

"Those were beavers, my dear. What's for lunch?"

Chapter Eight

After lunch, Belle decided to accept Skye's offer to visit her veterinary clinic and left with Skye, Napoleon and Gus.

As they headed for the car, Belle asked, "Where is your clinic?"

"Just beyond that grove of trees," Skye said, pointing west.

"That close? Tell you what, I need some exercise. I think I'll walk over."

Skye hesitated for a moment. "Gus and I'll walk with you."

"That's not necessary if it makes you uncomfortable," Belle said. "He didn't go into particulars, but Gabe told me that you had some security issues."

"I'll be fine. Napoleon can drive behind us." Skye nodded to Napoleon, who got in the Jeep.

"I hope that you'll feel safe with me," Belle said. "Remember my training. I've handled some pretty tough customers in my day. Want me to go get my gun?"

Skye's eyes widened. "You have a *gun?*"

"Of course. It's a standard part of being an agent, and I still carry one. How about you?"

"Nope," Skye said as they walked toward the clinic. "I never learned to shoot. Guns make me nervous."

"They're certainly to be respected, but, these days, lots of women are learning to shoot and carrying guns for security, especially when they travel. My father's a sheriff, so I've been around guns all my life. By the time I was a teenager, I could shoot a redbug off a fence post." Belle smiled at the memory. "Those were my dad's words."

Skye smiled. "He sounds like a character."

"He is."

"Growing up in a big family must have been fun."

"It had its moments," Belle said. "But sometimes it seemed as if I had six parents bossing me around—or trying to. And it was noisy. Privacy was hard to come by."

By the time they reached the clinic, Belle was breathing hard. Boy, was she out of shape. Before her bout with pneumonia, she could have run five miles and not have been so winded.

Napoleon pulled into one of the parking spaces in front and went to unlock the heavily carved door to the clinic. The building was the same limestone as the main house and roofed with red Spanish tiles.

Belle started forward, but Skye put her hand on Belle's arm. "Wait here while Napoleon disables the alarm and checks things."

"Unless there's a crazed rhinoceros loose in there, I can handle anything else we might meet," Belle said. "I also have a black belt in karate. Come on."

Skye giggled and followed. "I believe you could handle a crazed rhinoceros, too."

Belle winked. "You may be right."

Inside, Skye showed Belle around the clinic. The waiting room was furnished with rustic pieces that didn't come from a junkyard, for sure. She wondered if Lisa, the decorator shark, had worked her magic here as well? The examining rooms were all pristine chrome and leather. Beautiful landscapes hung on the walls—mostly Flora's, she suspected. In a back room were several cages. Two were occupied by cats.

Skye took one out and cuddled her. "This young lady was here for surgery. She's going home this afternoon."

The calico hissed a bit at Gus, but the dog, who'd never left Skye's side, only yawned and stretched out on the floor.

"Settle down, Buttons," Skye said softly. The cat relaxed. "The other is staying with us for a few days while her owner is in the hospital."

"Oh, do you board animals?"

"Only a few and under special circumstances. Inside here, we tend to the small animals. Outside in back are facilities for larger animals—like crazed rhinos."

Belle laughed. "Or horses."

"Or horses. Or cows. Or goats."

"Or llamas. So you treat everything?" Belle asked.

"Yes, but mostly I see small animals. Dogs, cats, ferrets, skunks, that sort of thing."

"Skunks?"

Skye shrugged. "Not my first choice for a pet, either."

"You must have had some interesting cases."

"I have. Ever try to do CPR on a goldfish?"

"Not lately. Was it successful?"

"Nope. Goldie was long gone to fishy heaven when Jenny

insisted that her mother bring it in to see me. Instead, I presided at the funeral."

"I've buried many a goldfish of my own. Did you sing at the service?"

"Napoleon did that. He has a beautiful voice. We have a small pet cemetery on the property and a standard funeral ritual that we perform occasionally."

"You're kidding."

"Nope."

"Did you have to go to divinity school to do that?"

Skye laughed. "Not hardly. But I did have our minister help me write the service. It's very sweet and simple."

"When we lost a pet, we usually buried them out in the pasture and said our own words over them."

"Most people do the same here, but—" Skye was interrupted by her cell phone. She pulled it from her pocket and answered it. "Oh, Judy, I'm sorry. No, no, don't worry about it. I'm sure Suki can fill in. I'll see you Monday."

Skye looked troubled, so Belle said, "Problems?"

"That was our afternoon receptionist. Judy's car won't start, and she's waiting on road service to come and take a look at it. She's a student at the university in San Marcos, very conscientious and extremely frustrated right now. I need to call Suki. Our first appointment is in about five minutes."

"I'll be happy to help," Belle said. "Tell me what to do."

Skye frowned. "Are you sure you're up to it?"

"Of course. My telephone skills aren't bad, and I like animals."

Skye laughed. "I meant do you feel like it? Gabe will kill me if I put you to work and exhaust you."

"I can't see Gabe killing you, and I'd welcome the chance to do something useful."

"Then you're on. But you have to promise me that if you begin to get too tired, you'll let me know."

"Cross my heart," Belle said, drawing an *X* on her chest.

Just after Skye quickly explained the receptionist's job, the phone rang, and Skye answered. She informed the gate guard that Belle would be filling in for Judy. To Belle, she said, "Mrs. Albritton is on her way with Mimi, her toy poodle. I'll go get things set up. Be sure to check through the spy hole before you let them in and check that the door is locked after they're inside."

"Gotcha." The security measures seem obsessive, but Belle bit her tongue and didn't question them.

In a few minutes, the doorbell rang and Belle ushered in an older woman with curly white hair carrying a tiny poodle with curly white hair.

"Mrs. Albritton, I'm Belle, filling in for Judy this afternoon. I'll let the doctor know that you're here."

"Oh, you must be the houseguest," the woman said. "The one from Colorado."

Belle was startled at first, then remembered the speed of the grapevine in small towns. "Yes, I am."

By mid-afternoon, Belle's energy was running low. There had been a steady stream of appointments, and she'd been busy answering the phone and letting each patient in and out, as well as doing the billing. She'd even mopped the floor when a nervous Doberman puppy piddled on it.

When the bell rang in between appointments, she peered through the hole and was surprised to see Gabe and Suki.

Belle opened the door. "Do you have an appointment?"

Gabe grinned. "We're the reinforcements."

"We don't need reinforcements. We're doing just fine."

"Huh!" Suki said. "You don't look fine to me. You look like you've been pulled through a knothole backwards."

"That bad?"

"Well, maybe a bit this side of that bad, but your eyes are all droopy, and you look plum tuckered out. You run along with Gabe, and I'll take over here." Suki marched over to the receptionist's cubicle.

Belle looked at Gabe and he shrugged. "I've learned not to argue with her. And you do look tired. It's past your nap time. Come on. I'll drive you back."

She didn't argue. She was too tired.

She must have fallen asleep the minute her head leaned back against the seat because the next thing she knew, Gabe was trying to lift her from the car.

"What are you doing?" she asked, shoving him away.

"I was going to carry you upstairs."

"Are you out of your mind? You'd throw your back out."

He laughed. "You wound me. I was trying to be gallant."

"Then toss your jacket on the ground, but don't get a hernia trying to lug me around like a baby. I'm a hundred and thirty pounds of solid muscle."

"Yes, ma'am." Gabe quickly peeled off his sport coat and fanned it on the ground.

"Oh, good grief!" Belle snatched up his coat and brushed it off. "Your dry cleaning bills must be outrageous."

"I get a special deal. The dry cleaner is a sucker for romance. And he's my partner."

"You own a dry cleaner's?"

"Half of one—the silent half. Come on. Let's get you in bed."

If Belle hadn't been so tired, she wouldn't have let his last comment ride, but, truth was, she was pooped. And when he started up the stairs with her, she stopped him.

"I can take it from here."

"Sure you don't need any help?"

Belle glared. "I can manage my jammies just fine."

"Oops. Sorry. I was coddling, wasn't I?"

"You were."

"I'll work on it. Thanks for helping Skye this afternoon."

"I enjoyed doing it. I'm not used to sitting around being idle."

"Want to go horseback riding tomorrow morning—if the doctor okays it?"

"Sure," Belle said. "I'd love to, but I don't need the doctor's okay. She just said take things easy. I'm not an invalid, Gabe."

"Yes, ma'am."

She cocked an eyebrow. "You're going to call her anyway, aren't you?"

"Yep."

"You're certainly hardheaded."

"That's what your brother says about you."

She laughed. "He's right."

"Western or English?"

"Western."

"You have any boots?"

"Of course I have boots." Then she remembered. "But they're at Sam's."

"You can probably borrow a pair of Skye's or Mom's. What size do you wear?"

"Eight and a half narrow. Bigger than either of them, I imagine. But I can wear my athletic shoes. I used to ride barefoot half the time."

"I'll check. Have a nice nap."

She did. Belle practically died when her head touched the pillow, and she slept until it was time to go downstairs for dinner. She would have liked nothing better than to have stayed in her room curled up in her sleep shirt with a book and a pimento cheese sandwich. Gabe's family and the others in the household had been supernice to her, but all the togetherness was wearing on her.

ANTICIPATING A RIDE, Belle awoke earlier than usual the following morning and dressed in jeans and a sweatshirt. Everyone, except Flora, was at breakfast, and they greeted her as she took her place and poured a first cup of coffee.

"You look a right smart more pert this morning," Suki said.

"I'm feeling a right smart more pert," Belle said.

"I hope I didn't tire you out too much yesterday," Skye said, looking concerned. "I wanted to thank you again for stepping in to help."

"You've already thanked me enough," Belle said. "I enjoyed having something to do."

The doorbell rang, and Skye got up. "That must be Napoleon."

"You work on Saturday?" Belle asked.

"Until noon. See you later."

Ralph said, "I'll see you to the door and be out about my business."

"We usually have pancakes on Saturday morning," Suki

said to Belle. "I've kept some warm in the kitchen. Or I can get you some of that stuff with the nuts and seeds."

"Pancakes would be great." Belle rose. "I can get them."

"Keep your seat. I've got to take this stack of dishes to the kitchen anyway. You want bacon or sausage? Or some of that fake tofu stuff that Skye passes off as sausage?"

"I'll try the tofu."

"It don't taste like good pork sausage to me, but if that's what you want, that's what you'll get." Gathering a stack of dishes, she hurried off to the kitchen.

Looking amused, Gabe had watched the exchange. "It's really not that bad. Suki's just set in her ways."

"I heard that, Gabriel Burrell," Suki called from the kitchen.

He only laughed. "Want to read the *Wimberley Star* with your breakfast?" He held out the paper, which consisted of one section with no more than a dozen pages.

"Anything interesting going on?"

"Well, let's see. The New Neighbors are having a salad luncheon next Wednesday, the Texans won the basketball game, the Village sales tax revenues are up slightly for the month, and somebody is starting a pottery class on Monday."

"Let me see that."

"Does the salad luncheon interest you?"

"No, but the pottery class does. I've always wanted to learn to do that. I loved making mud pies when I was a kid."

"I used to love watching Charlie throw pots. He even let me try it, but I wasn't very good. He had the patience of Job."

"Charlie?"

"Charlie Walker, my stepfather."

"Oh, yes," Belle said. "Skye's father. Do you have any of his work?"

"It's all over the house. Almost everything that's ceramic is his, including our dinnerware."

"And including that marvelous big bowl on my coffee table and the vase on my dresser?"

"All his."

"I'm impressed. Did you and Skye inherit any artistic abilities?"

"Nope. Skye has a way with animals, and I have a knack for business—which is good. Early on I learned that Charlie and my mother were undervaluing their art, so I did some research and made them raise their prices."

"How old were you?"

"About twelve."

"Child prodigy," Belle said as Suki returned with a plate.

"Who?" Suki said.

"Gabe. Thanks for the pancakes, Suki. And the fake sausage. Looks good." She poured syrup over the pancakes and dug in. "Umm. These are wonderful."

"Thanks," Gabe said.

"Did you make these?"

"I did. One of my few culinary skills. I added milk and eggs and followed the directions on the box. Still want to go riding this morning?"

"Of course."

"I'll call Manuel and tell him to have the horses saddled for us."

While Belle ate, Gabe called on his cell phone.

"Oh, by the way," Belle said, "I've been meaning to ask if there's a car rental agency in Wimberley."

"Afraid not. The closest one is in San Marcos. Why?"

"I'd like to rent a car."

"To go where?"

Belle felt a flash of irritation. "Wherever I want to go."

"I can take you anywhere you want to go. Is there some place in particular that interests you?"

"Yes, the rental agency in San Marcos. Can you take me there this afternoon?"

Gabe looked concerned. "Are you planning on leaving?"

"Eventually. Or am I a prisoner here?"

Gabe frowned. "What are you talking about?"

"Gabe, I'm an adult woman, and I have been for some time. I like to be able to come and go when it suits me. My vehicle is at Sam's place, so I'd like to have a temporary replacement."

"I understand. Sorry if I sounded like a concerned papa. There's no need to rent a car. We have half a dozen or more around here, and the keys are on a board out by the freezers. Pick any one you want. Take the blue Lexus if you like."

"Isn't that your car?"

"I'll drive the black one or one of the SUVs. Honestly, there are plenty of vehicles around here without your having to rent another one."

She considered being hard-nosed about it simply on general principle, then she reneged. While she had a nice financial cushion from the oil lease money of the Naconiche property, it might have to do her for a while. Rental cars could add up in a hurry. "Thanks. I'll take you up on the offer."

"Good." He slapped his thighs and stood. "Let's go riding."

"I'm ready."

"Let me get something from my room first. I'll meet you in the foyer."

Chapter Nine

"Boots?" Belle said. "You got me new boots?"

"Yep," Gabe said. "You like them?"

"What's not to like? But they're eelskin."

"Makes them soft. Try them on and see if they fit."

The boots fit as if they'd been custom-made. A lovely caramel color, they were butter soft and gorgeous. And obviously very expensive. "If you'll give me the bill, I'll pay you for them."

"Not necessary."

"I insist."

"No. Consider them a birthday present."

"My birthday is in January."

He grinned. "Then I'm a little late or very early." He opened the hall closet and took out two cowboy hats, a white one and a red one. "One is Mom's and one is Skye's. See which one fits best."

Wouldn't you know that the red one was perfect. "Flora's?"

"How did you guess?"

"Just a hunch. Where's your hat?"

"Right here." He took another white one off a hook and settled it on his head, the brim pulled low over his eyes.

"You look like a regular cowboy." And he did. Ruggedly handsome and all man in his scuffed boots and worn jeans. Blame it on her early conditioning, but she'd always been a sucker for cowboy boots and well-filled jeans.

"I *am* a regular cowboy." He put his hand to her back. "Ready?"

"Raring to go."

Outside, a Jeep sat by the front steps.

"Is the stable so far that we have to drive?" Belle asked.

"Not far at all. But let's save our energy for the ride."

"Which is a fancy way of saying that I'm too puny to do a little walking. Gabe, I'm not. And I need the exercise. I'm used to running at least a couple of miles a day as well as weight training. If I don't soon get back into some sort of regimen, I'm going to be horribly out of shape."

"Your shape looks great to me."

Big eye roll.

"Tell you what," he said, "we'll talk to Dr. Hamilton again on Monday, and if she okays it, you can use my weight room."

"You have a weight room?"

"I do. A well-equipped one." He steered her to the Jeep and opened the door. "I have every machine known to man—or woman. You're welcome to take your pick. And we'll ask her about swimming as well. Do you swim?"

"Of course I swim, but isn't it still a little chilly for swimming?"

"Not if you have a heated pool."

"You mean that lovely pool off the back patio is *heated?* Why didn't you tell me sooner?"

"Do you have a suit?"

"Well, not with me, but I can buy one. Or maybe I can borrow one from your mother."

Gabe peered at her from under the brim of his hat. "I don't think hers would fit, and Skye doesn't swim."

"Can't or doesn't?"

"Doesn't. She used to be a regular fish."

"Why doesn't she swim anymore?"

"I don't think she likes to get her hair wet."

Skye didn't impress her as the type to care much about her hairdo, so his answer struck her as just so much bull, but she let it pass. They drove a short distance to the stables, where two horses were waiting for them. The smaller, a roan with white stockings, reminded her of Sunset.

"Oh, aren't you a beauty?" Belle said, giving the mare a pat. "What's your name?"

"She's Letty, and this is Thunder. Climb up and let me check your stirrups." He made a step of his hands.

"I can check my own stirrups, and I don't need a boost." Belle climbed into the saddle in one easy motion. "They're fine."

"Good. The ground is rocky around here, so stick to the paths," Gabe said as he mounted.

"Gotcha." Belle was tempted to take off at a fast clip, but she beat back the urge and rode at a sedate pace beside Gabe. She'd spent a good part of her earlier years galloping across the pastures and along the rural roads of Naconiche County with her brothers or alone, so she was no stranger to horses. She'd mucked out many a stall in Texas and Colorado.

They rode at a granny pace for ten or fifteen minutes—until Belle couldn't stand it anymore. She resettled the red hat on her head, yelled, "Race you!" and took off like greased lightning.

Laughing, she bent low over Letty's neck as the mare responded. "Good girl!"

She glanced over her shoulder to find that Gabe was gaining fast. The mare wasn't a match for the big brute he rode, so she slowed, then pulled up.

"What the hell are you doing?" Gabe shouted when he stopped beside her and grabbed her reins.

Her eyes widened. "I beg your pardon?"

"You could have gotten yourself killed!"

"On a horse? I don't think so. With equal mounts, I could ride bareback and beat you any day of the week."

He glared at her for a minute, then his expression softened and morphed into a smile. "You probably could."

"No probably to it. I was practically born on a horse."

"I'll bet you gave your mother fits when you were a little girl."

Belle joined him in a smile. "I did."

They rode for another half hour or so before Gabe insisted they call it quits for the day. She was reluctant but finally agreed.

Manuel met them at the stable.

Belle threw up the stirrup and reached for the cinch to unsaddle her horse, when Manuel hurried to her, looking alarmed. "No, no, senorita. I will do that."

She glanced to Gabe, who nodded. Dear Lord, deliver her from male egos.

On the drive back to the house, she said, "Thanks. I really enjoyed that."

"I could tell."

"Is Letty Skye's horse?"

He nodded. "But she doesn't ride her much."

"Don't tell me. Her hair."

Gabe smiled. "Could be. Hat hair is a terrible thing."

"I don't believe for a minute that Skye is that concerned about her hair. Why doesn't she ride?"

"Actually, I think she's simply too busy these days. By the time she's seen her last patient, it's dark or nearly so. Maybe when the days are longer, she'll be able to ride."

Sounded plausible. But she didn't believe that story, either. Something bad must have really spooked Skye to make her stay behind locked doors most of the time. Belle didn't know how she stood it. She'd been here less than a week, and she was going stir-crazy.

Gabe must have read her mind. "Say, want to drive to San Marcos for dinner and a movie tonight?"

"Sounds great, but doesn't Wimberley have a movie theater?"

"Nope. We have a walk-in, but it doesn't open until Memorial Day."

"A walk-in?"

"It's like a drive-in but without the car. From Memorial Day to Labor Day, we have an open-air theater that shows first-run pictures at night."

"In Naconiche, the mosquitoes would carry you off."

"They're pretty bad around here, too, but they offer bug spray with each ticket."

She cocked her head. "Are you pulling my leg?"

"No, but I'll give it a shot if you're game."

"You're crazy, Gabe Burrell," she said, laughing. "What time do we leave?"

"We'll check the schedule when we get home."

BELLE PULLED ON the blue one-piece suit and looked in the mirror. It fit perfectly. She'd talked Gabe into driving over to San Marcos a little early so that she could find a swimsuit. The pickings were slim so early in the spring, but this one would do.

"Does it fit?" Flora asked from outside the cubicle.

Belle opened the door. "What do you think?"

"Lovely, dear, but try this one, too." She held up a red bikini that was little more than strings. "Red is your color."

There was hardly enough fabric to make an adequate color sample, but rather than argue, Belle took the suit and tried it. Wearing it in public might get her arrested, but she decided to take both suits.

Flora seemed extremely pleased.

"Where's Gabe?" Belle asked after she'd paid for her purchase.

"Over by the fishing lures I think. That man loves to fish."

Gabe had insisted that his mother come along with them. He would have brought Skye, Suki and Ralph if they would have come. Skye refused, saying that she needed to work on an article she was writing for a vet journal, and Suki and Ralph begged off as well—to stay home and babysit Skye, Belle figured. Flora's presence effectively squelched any idea Belle might have had that this was a date. Which, she was sure, was Gabe's intention. Fine with her. But, boy, was he sending mixed messages.

They had dinner at a great seafood restaurant and went to the movie they'd selected.

Belle had been amused at the musical chair game that Gabe and Flora played at the theater. Gabe maneuvered so that Flora sat between them. He was slick, but his mother was slicker.

"Belle, dear, would you change seats with me? Gabe's aftershave is giving me a headache."

"It's the same brand I always use," Gabe said.

"Sorry, dear," Flora said, patting Gabe's thigh. "Maybe it was the trout I ate."

Gabe looked bewildered, as she and Flora switched places.

Belle leaned over to Gabe and whispered, "I think your aftershave smells very good. But then, I had shrimp."

He chuckled. "Sorry about that. Sometimes my mother doesn't make much sense."

Flora made perfect sense. She was matchmaking again.

The movie was terrific—a funny and warm, feel-good story that left Belle upbeat and smiling all the way home.

The only thing missing was a good-night kiss. From Gabe. Flora gave her one just inside the foyer and hurried upstairs before the door closed.

"Thank you for this evening," Belle said. "I really enjoyed myself."

"You're welcome. I enjoyed it, too. By the way, we'll be going to early church services in the morning. You can come with us or sleep in, your choice."

"I really don't have church clothes with me. I think I'll pass this time."

"No problem." He touched the small of her back and walked with her to the foot of the stairs. "Good night."

She felt him hesitate. Her every instinct screamed that he wanted to kiss her.

He didn't. He didn't move.

She wanted to grab his shirt, drag his mouth to hers and kiss him senseless.

Dumb idea. Very dumb.

But the urge grew stronger.

Quickly, she decided to compromise. She tiptoed and pecked his cheek. "Good night and thanks again." She ran upstairs before her urge got out of hand.

THE HOUSE WAS QUIET when Belle stuck her head out her door the next morning. Figuring that everyone was at church, she decided to go for a quick dip in the pool before she dressed and had her coffee. She wore the red bikini and wrapped a towel around her in sarong style.

She was halfway down the stairs when the doorbell rang.

Who could that be?

She trotted to the front door and peered through the peephole.

A large, soulful eye peered back at her.

Carlotta. She'd escaped again.

Belle considered ignoring the llama, but the doorbell rang again.

Oh, good grief! She flung open the door, meaning to shoo Carlotta off the porch and take her back to the pasture. Carlotta had other ideas. And, worse, Belle had forgotten to check the alarm. It went off with a raucous *brrrrng* that reverberated through the house.

The llama made a lunge for the foyer. Belle tried to close the door but only managed to trap Carlotta's head and neck.

Shoving on her head to push her out didn't work, and there was no way she could stop shoving to turn off the alarm. She threw her whole weight into keeping the door from opening wider and allowing the animal inside. Unfortunately, Belle was standing on an area rug, and Carlotta was hell-bent on coming into the house.

The rug started to scoot backward and accordion up as Carlotta gained headway, pitting her determination to get in against Belle's efforts to keep her out. Where was help when she needed it?

"Carlotta! Stop it! Stop it! You can't come in."

Carlotta only seemed to smile and kept shoving. The alarm kept ringing. The rug, and Belle with it, kept scooting backward.

Why hadn't she thought to bring a banana or Suki's broom?

Tiger came running downstairs, yapping and running around Belle's feet. "Go away, Tiger!" Tiger didn't listen. He only increased his barking, directed at Carlotta now.

Carlotta didn't appreciate the barking, either; it only seemed to give her an extra surge of power as she thrust against the door.

The rug scooted backward more and more until Belle was almost horizontal, feet on the floor and hands on the door, and the animal was halfway inside. "Stop, Carlotta! Dammit, don't do this!"

The llama gave one final lunge, and Belle fell flat as Carlotta scrambled inside and ran for the back of the house. A table toppled; a vase of tulips crashed against the tile floor; a chair went awry.

Belle jumped to her feet and chased her, screaming and turning the air blue. Tiger scurried after the llama as well, yapping incessantly and adding to the noisy confusion. Belle's towel came loose, and she grabbed it as she ran. Now that she was inside, Carlotta seemed confused and frightened of the house. Belle grabbed her around the neck, but it was worse than wrestling a Brahma bull, and she couldn't hang on.

Flapping the towel, Belle tried to herd her back to the open front door, but the llama only became more skittish, banging into this and that and ending up in the kitchen. She headed straight for the big wooden fruit bowl on the island. Her nudging sent the bowl rocking and skittering until it slammed to the floor, and fruit went flying in all directions.

"Hold it right there!" a deep voice shouted.

A big guy with a buzz cut stood in the doorway, a shotgun aimed at her.

"I'm a guest here!" Belle shouted back. "Put that blasted gun down and help me with this animal!"

The man looked bewildered, but he put the twelve-gauge on the bar. "What do you want me to do?"

"When she runs your way, grab her ears and hold on."

Belle flapped the towel, herding Carlotta toward the guard. He grabbed an ear in each hand and held on. Carlotta hissed and spit, but he held her. Yapping and growling, Tiger grabbed hold of the man's pant cuff and began tugging.

"Stop it, Tiger!"

Tiger didn't listen any better than Carlotta. At least with his mouth full of khaki, the Yorkie had to stop his yapping.

Quickly, Belle reached for the man's thick leather belt and started unbuckling it.

"Lady! What are you doing?"

"I'm making a strap to go around her neck," Belle yelled

over the noise of the jarring alarm and the unruly llama. "Don't let her go."

She rebuckled the belt around Carlotta's neck and threw the towel over her head to blind her. Grabbing a half-smashed banana from the floor, Belle peeled it back, pinched off a piece and held it to Carlotta's mouth. The llama sniffed, then nibbled the morsel.

"Okay, grab the belt and let's see if we can coax her outside."

"Can you get this dog off my leg?"

"Tiger! Stop. Sit."

Wonder of wonders, Tiger obeyed. Tail wagging, he sat and cocked his head, looking very proud of himself.

They started moving the llama out of the kitchen. They'd made it to the foyer when a car screeched to a stop outside, and Gabe came bounding up the steps.

"What's going on?" Gabe shouted.

"Do we look like we're having a tea party?" Belle shouted back. "We're trying to get this creature out of the house!"

Gabe looked as if he were about to break into riotous laughter.

"Don't you dare laugh, Gabe Burrell! If you laugh, I swear I'll get my gun and shoot you on the spot."

"Yes, ma'am." Hurriedly, he went to the box and turned off the alarm.

Blessed quiet helped calm her jangled nerves.

"Here," Gabe said, "Dwayne and I will get Carlotta back into the pasture."

Belle didn't argue. She thrust the banana at him and closed the door after they managed to half wrestle, half coax the animal onto the porch.

She up-righted the table and the chair and straightened

the foyer rug, then sat down in the chair to catch her breath and survey the damage. The tiles were strewn with crushed tulips and glass, water and nervous llama droppings.

And that was just the foyer. She shuddered to think of what else she and Carlotta had broken during their escapade through the house. What if priceless art objects had been damaged?

Sucking in a fortifying breath, she stood and went to find a broom and survey the damage.

Chapter Ten

After he and the guard got the llama back into the pasture, Gabe said, "Dwayne, take my car and go wait for the family outside the church. They should be getting out in about ten or fifteen minutes."

"Yes, sir. Soon as I get my shotgun."

"What happened to your gun?"

"I left it in the kitchen when I went inside to see what set off the alarm. I didn't know your guest was there. Hope I didn't scare her."

Gabe chuckled. "Not likely. She's an ex-FBI agent."

Dwayne's eyes widened. "You're kidding. For real?"

"For real."

"She sure don't look like any FBI agent I ever saw. Did you get a load of her in that— Sorry, sir. I forgot she was your guest."

"That's okay, Dwayne. Be hard to miss. Let's get your gun."

When they opened the front door, Belle was squatted on the floor, still in her bikini but now sporting a pair of yellow rubber gloves, shoveling flowers and glass into a garbage bag. She was a sight to behold.

It took him a couple of seconds to get words out of his mouth. "Dwayne wanted to get his gun."

Belle glanced up. "It's leaning in the corner there. I removed the shell from the chamber. Thanks for your help, Dwayne, is it?"

Dwayne, who was bug-eyed, swallowed and said, "Yes, ma'am. Glad to help." He didn't budge from his spot.

"Better retrieve your gun and get moving, Dwayne."

The young man turned beet-red. "Yes, sir." He grabbed his shotgun and beat a quick retreat.

Gabe hardly felt like playing the gentleman, either. He forced himself to look away, take off his jacket and toss it on a chair. "If you want to run upstairs and change, I'll finish that."

"It's okay. I've got most of it."

"Uh, Belle, your top has…shifted."

She froze, then glanced down. "Ohmygod!" She slapped her arms across her chest, jumped up and ran upstairs.

Gabe regretted that he'd had to embarrass her, but he'd be lying if he said he'd regretted the circumstances. He'd spent more than one sleepless night thinking about Belle and that lovely body. The reality of her breasts was even better than his imagination.

Before he allowed himself to dwell on her breasts any longer and become more aroused than he already was, he grabbed a roll of paper towels sitting on the hall table to finish cleaning up.

Lord, she was gorgeous.

BELLE FLUNG the rubber gloves against the bathroom mirror, stripped off the red bikini and threw it in the trash. She'd always been comfortable with her body and not overly modest, but she'd never been into flashing, either. This ranked at the top of her list of most embarrassing moments. No wonder the guard was gawking. And Gabe. How would she ever be able to face him again? She wanted to crawl in bed and pull the covers over her head. The only thing that would have been worse was if the whole family had been there. Thank heaven for small miracles.

She quickly dressed in jeans and a T-shirt, sneaked downstairs and, after peeking over the banister to check if the foyer was clear, hurried outside. She ought to be in the kitchen cleaning the mess in there, but she wasn't that brave. Which was stupid. Why the major uproar?

She'd been embarrassed, sure, but she'd been embarrassed before and survived. Why couldn't she just laugh and blow it off? Showing a little boob wasn't a threat to world peace. What Gabe Burrell and some kid thought wasn't that big a deal.

Or was it?

What about it bothered her so?

Gabe bothered her. Like it or not, he bothered her in a big way. A shame she hadn't met him before she got tangled up with Matt. But she hadn't, and no way was she going to start thinking hearts-and-flowers stuff before she'd had time to get her head straight again. He was just a friend. Just a friend, she reminded herself.

Some distance from the house, she pulled a stalk of grass, climbed on a limestone boulder and began chewing on the stalk as she gazed off in the distance. She ought to leave here and go to Naconiche. When she'd talked to her folks a couple of nights ago, she didn't tell them about the divorce. She'd only mentioned something vague about needing to spend some time away from Colorado and that she'd gotten sick and was staying with friends in Wimberley. Belle could tell that her mother's feelings were hurt that she hadn't come home.

Home? Naconiche didn't seem like home anymore. Her brother Frank and his family lived in the place where she'd grown up. Her parents' apartment over the Double Dip certainly wasn't home. The home she'd thought was hers in Colorado was gone. She didn't feel as if she belonged anywhere.

She didn't have a home; she didn't have a career; she didn't even have friends anymore. She'd left everything behind.

Luckily she had a family. A wonderful, loving family. But she wasn't ready to see them yet. She had to regain her strength and get a few things straight in her head first. Like figuring out what she wanted to do with the rest of her life. Her oil-lease money wouldn't last forever.

"Ah, there you are," Gabe said from behind her. "What are you doing out here?"

"Considering my options," she said without turning around.

"Which are?"

"Slitting my wrists, wearing a sack over my head or stealing a car and making a fast getaway."

"They all sound like lousy options to me. Why consider those?"

"Because I'm embarrassed. And I've embarrassed you."

"Good Lord, I wasn't embarrassed. Caught off guard maybe, mesmerized for sure, but not embarrassed." He climbed up on the boulder and put his arm around her. "I feel terrible that you had to contend with such an ordeal when all you wanted to do was go swimming. What happened?"

"The doorbell rang. When I saw it was Carlotta, I was going to shoo her away, but she got in and the alarm went off and chaos ensued."

"I think the whole mess is Skye's fault."

Surprised, Belle said, "Skye's fault?"

"Sure. If she hadn't taught that dumb llama how to ring the doorbell, none of this would have happened."

Belle laughed. "Carlotta's not dumb. She's very smart. I'm dumb for forgetting about the alarm."

"No, my mother's dumb for setting the alarm."

"*Flora* set the alarm?"

"No, I did, but I'd rather blame it on somebody else."

"You're crazy," Belle said, laughing and bumping against him.

"I am. You seem to have that effect on me, Miss Belle Starr Outlaw." He kissed her nose, then moved lower to her mouth.

Lightly, he brushed his lips back and forth against hers. Teasing, offering, inviting more. Every time they got that close together, some sort of magnetic force seemed to kick in, drawing them closer, fogging her brain.

Maybe she shouldn't have accepted the invitation and kissed him, but she did. Foolish choice, really foolish choice, but it felt wonderful.

He had the warmest lips.

His cell phone rang.

"Damn!" Gabe said, but he answered it. After a brief conversation, he said, "That was Mother. Brunch is ready. Hungry?"

"I could eat. What are we having?"

"Fruit salad from bruised fruit."

She laughed, and they headed back to the house.

"By the way," Gabe said, "I saw Dr. Hamilton at church this morning. She said you were okay to drive when you felt like it, but you might want to hold off any NASCAR racing for a while."

"Oh, shoot. My team will be disappointed."

ON MONDAY MORNING, Belle got up at a decent hour and was downstairs before Gabe and Skye left for work.

Gabe looked up from his newspaper as she sat down at the table. "Good morning. You're up bright and early today."

"I decided it was time I stopped being a slug. Besides, I start my classes today."

"What classes?" Skye asked, pouring a mug of coffee for Belle and another for herself.

"Ceramics for starters. There are several different things that begin this week. I figured that I'd ask around and register for whatever sounded interesting. I may even take bridge lessons or creative writing."

"Need a ride?" Gabe asked. "The center is near my office."

"Thanks, but I'd like to drive if you don't mind my borrowing a car. I thought I might do a bit of exploring while I'm out."

"Help yourself. You know where the keys are."

Suki came in from the kitchen. "'Mornin'," she said, nodding to Belle. "You want some eggs or cereal?"

"Cereal's fine," Belle said, noting that Suki was already carrying a bowl.

"How long are the classes?" Skye asked.

"I understand that there's quite a variation. Some meet two or three times for two weeks, others meet once a week for six weeks. But don't worry. I don't plan to hang around underfoot for six weeks. I figured that I'd just go get a feel for some different subjects. I doubt that anyone would get upset if I quit after a couple of sessions, especially if I'm paying for lessons in advance."

"We'd love to have you stay for six weeks—or six months for that matter," Gabe said. "Or longer if you'd like."

"Of course," Skye said. "We enjoy having you here."

Belle felt as if they were sincere, but she didn't feel comfortable intruding into their household.

"You're not one bit of trouble," Suki said, as if she'd read Belle's mind. "And Carlotta's taken quite a shine to you." She let out a cackle of laughter as she went back to the kitchen.

"I'm so sorry about Carlotta," Skye said. "I should have never taught her to ring the doorbell. It seemed funny at the time."

"No problem," Belle said. "And you've apologized enough already. I'm only glad we didn't break anything terribly valuable. I would have been horrified if one of your dad's pieces had gotten broken. They're so beautiful."

"Aren't they? It's a shame I didn't inherit his talent."

Napoleon arrived just then, and Skye left for the clinic. Gabe rose as well. "I have an appointment with a client," he said, "so I'd better get a move on. Don't tire yourself today."

"Yes, Mother."

Gabe chuckled, then bent and surprised her with a quick kiss. "See you later."

She should have said something then, but he seemed in a hurry, so she didn't, but the kiss seemed altogether too familiar. They needed to have a serious talk about boundaries and intentions.

THE CENTER WASN'T OVERRUN with people, but several were already assembled, ready to sign up. She even recognized two of them—the Misses Culbertson. Alma and Thelma, the retired teachers that she'd met at the doctor's office. Today they were in pants and neatly pressed oxford shirts, one pink and one blue.

"Why, good morning," Alma said. Or was it Thelma? She wore the pink shirt. "Are you taking a class?"

"One or more," Belle said. "I hope there's room left in the ceramics section."

"I think there is," the other twin said. "That's what we're taking. Just sign your name on the sheet and give Mary Sue your fifteen dollars. We get a price break since we're senior citizens. I hope you don't mind having a class with all us old fogies."

Belle smiled. "Not at all. I enjoy people of all ages." She signed her name on the list and gave a check to the white-haired lady behind the desk—Mary Sue she assumed. She also picked up a schedule of various classes being offered. Bridge, she noticed, was full, and mah-jongg didn't interest her. Nor did portfolio planning for retirement, or line dancing. Yoga was a possibility, as was creative writing and flower arranging. She'd always meant to take yoga and never had, so she signed up for it, too. Creative writing? Why not? She added her name to that list as well. She'd have to think about the flower arranging. Her schedule was getting full. Ceramics was on Monday and Wednesday mornings, creative writing on Tuesday evenings, and yoga on Thursday morning. That was enough for now, though it would be nice to learn how to arrange flowers in a vase and have them not look as if they'd just been stuck there. Her mother had been really good at it.

"What else did you sign up for?" asked Alma/Thelma as they walked together to room four.

"Creative writing and yoga," Belle said.

"Wonderful! We took yoga last session and had a delightful time. Sister and I love taking classes. It keeps our minds and bodies agile. Did I hear someone say that you were a spy? Fascinating. Absolutely fascinating."

Belle smiled. Word certainly had gotten around. "No, not a spy. I used to be an FBI agent."

"Do tell," said Thelma/Alma. "Why I'll wager if Mary Sue had known that, she would have enlisted you as an instructor in self-defense tactics. The person she had lined up moved to Waco."

"A real shame," the other twin said. "We wanted to take the class, too. Women can't be too careful these days. Do you carry a firearm, dear?"

"Frequently."

"So do we," Alma/Thelma whispered. "We took a class in firearms two years ago, and we've been packing ever since." She tittered. "We go to the firing range once a week to keep up our skills."

"You have a firing range in Wimberley?"

"Yes, indeed. And Wednesday nights ladies shoot for half price. Perhaps you'd like to come along with us and practice."

"Perhaps so."

"That would be grand. You can give us a few pointers."

They joined several others gathered along two paper-covered tables put together in a *V* shape. Their instructor, a middle-aged woman wearing smeared overalls and her salt-and-pepper hair in a ponytail, introduced herself as Molly Davis.

"I know most of you," Molly said, "but not all. Let's introduce ourselves. As I said, I'm Molly, and I'm a professional potter. I show here in Wimberley as well as galleries in Austin, Houston and Dallas."

"I'm Alma Culbertson," said the twin in the blue shirt. "I'm a retired elementary school teacher in the Wimberley Schools, and I believe that I know everybody here."

Alma, blue; Thelma, pink, Belle thought as Thelma introduced herself.

"I'm Belle Outlaw. I'm in Wimberley temporarily as a houseguest."

"She's staying with Flora Walker's family," Thelma added.

"Are you Gabe's fiancée?" a white-haired woman at the next table asked.

"Heavens, no, Esther," Thelma said. "That woman was the interior decorator, and she's old news. Belle is here recovering from a serious case of pneumonia. Her brother and Gabe Burrell are good friends."

At least she didn't mention that I was a spy, Belle thought.

Besides Esther, who was a recent widow "trying to find something to do with myself," the others were Katie, a young mother, and Roger, a spit-and-polish retired Air Force colonel.

The last member of the class was a young man in his twenties, who was in a wheelchair. "Steve Childs," he said, nodding briefly.

Molly launched into a brief history of ceramics, then passed out bib aprons to everyone. "I suggest that from now on everyone should wear old clothes that you don't mind getting dirty because art is a messy business. Today we're going to dive right in and get our hands dirty, so roll up your sleeves."

She handed each of them a ball of clay, and they started learning the vocabulary of ceramics as they beat and banged and folded and rolled. They made long snakes and shaped them into coiled pots, made clay pie crusts and cut pieces to shape a box, and spent a good bit of time on pinch pots. Pinch pots were formed by hand from a clay ball, begun by making an indentation with the thumbs and gradually pushing outward.

Belle noticed that she had to reball her clay and start over more than anyone else. Even Steve, who acted as if he didn't want to be there, was better at shaping than she was. But it was fun, and she finally made a pinch pot that was fairly decent. Class members left their boxes and pinch pots in the room to first air-dry, then be fired in a kiln. There wasn't room for the coil pots in the kiln, too, so everyone took theirs home to air-dry. Belle couldn't believe that class was over and two hours had flown by so quickly. It was almost noon.

As she and the Culbertsons walked down the hall, Alma said, "Thelma and I are going to Miguel's for lunch. Want to join us? On Mondays margaritas are free with the enchilada dinners. Their food is quite tasty."

Belle hesitated, then thought *What the heck.* "Sure, but let me call and tell Flora not to expect me. Are the others going?"

"Oh, no, dear," Thelma whispered. "Esther doesn't drink, and Katie has to pick up her daughter from kindergarten."

"And Roger has his men's group on Mondays," Alma added. "Do you like margaritas?"

With a straight face, Belle simply said, "Yes."

"Wonderful," the twins said in unison.

"What about Steve?"

"It didn't occur to me to ask," Alma said.

"I like margaritas," a voice behind them said.

Belle glanced back to see Steve behind them. "Frozen or on the rocks?"

"I'm not picky. And I like enchiladas, too. Beef, not the prissy kind with sour cream and chipotle sauce."

"Want to go have lunch with us at Miguel's?" Belle asked.

"Why the hell not? It's not like my appointment book is full. Want to ride with me in my van?"

"Sure," Belle said.

"Ladies?" He raised his eyebrows at the Misses Culbertson.

"Why, of course, Stephen," Alma said.

"We would be honored," Thelma added.

Outside, Belle phoned Gabe's house and talked to Suki while Steve activated the lift for his chair. She left her cell phone number in case she was needed for anything.

Alma and Thelma climbed into the backseat, and Belle got into the passenger side. When Steve got buckled up, he said, "Sorry about the mess. I wasn't expecting company."

"What mess?" Belle asked, ignoring the variety of empty cans, foam containers, assorted papers and clothing items.

Steve laughed for the first time. It was a nice laugh.

"Looks just the way your desk used to look," Alma said, "and I survived that."

"As did I," Thelma said. "I would have thought the Marines had taught you better neatness habits, Stephen."

He looked sheepish. "They did. I relapsed after…after I got out."

"Iraq?" Belle asked.

"Yes."

She nodded, understanding a great deal more about Steve than when she'd first met him.

The restaurant served great chips and salsa, very good enchiladas and excellent margaritas. Belle enjoyed spending time with Steve and the twins. They were a strange mixture of age and background, but they seemed to get along like old friends, trading stories and jokes until it was time to leave. Steve tried to get the check, but Alma insisted that they go Dutch.

"It's best that way," Thelma said. "After all, we're not wealthy." She glanced at Belle. "Unless you are, my dear."

"Hardly. I don't even have a job anymore."

"I'm sure that won't be a problem once you're fit again," Alma said on the way to the van.

"I hope not."

"Taking any other classes?" Steve asked Belle as he drove them back to the parking lot at the center.

"Creative writing and yoga."

"Me, too."

"You're taking yoga?"

He pulled into the parking lot and grinned. "No, only creative writing. It's hard to do the stork pose when you can't stand."

She let his comment pass. "Then I'll see you tomorrow night. Thanks for the ride." She said goodbye to the others and headed for Gabe's car.

Her cell phone rang as she was about to put the key in the ignition.

Gabe.

"We missed you at lunch. I hope you didn't have too many margaritas."

"Only the one freebie. But I had a nice time. Alma and Thelma are a hoot."

"You must have discovered a side of them that I'm not aware of. Want to do something exciting tonight after dinner?"

"Maybe. What did you have in mind?"

"Let me think about it," Gabe said, "and I'll try to come up with a plan."

Chapter Eleven

"Bingo!" Belle shouted.

"Are you sure?" Gabe asked. "That's your third one."

"Of course I'm sure. I've always been lucky at bingo."

When the checker verified her card, Belle smiled smugly at Gabe. "Told you." Her latest win was two tickets to a performance at the local playhouse. "Play your cards right and I'll take you along to the show."

"That's a deal."

"Belle, I wish you'd rub a little of your magic on me," Suki said. "I haven't even come close to winning all night."

"Nor have I," Flora said. "But I have a good feeling about this next one."

The entire household, including Suki, Ralph, Flora and even Skye and Gus, sat at a long table at the VFW hall for Monday night bingo. When Gabe had suggested doing something exciting after dinner, she'd had visions of boot scootin' at a local watering hole or attending a Willie Nelson concert in Austin. Something fun. And intimate. She hadn't expected to spend the evening with the family. Silly her.

One might think Gabe was deliberately avoiding being alone with her. Why?

Probably the same reason she was hesitant to be alone with him. The sparks between them seemed to be escalating. A simple touch on her back to guide her could send prickles zipping up her spine, and she often found herself daydreaming about his lips on hers.

"B thirteen, Belle," Suki said. "You've got that one."

"Oh, so I do." Belle turned her concentration back to the game.

A few minutes later, Suki jumped up, thrust her arms in the air and yelled, "Bingo! Bingo!"

Gabe leaned over and whispered, "See, I told you we'd do something exciting."

Before the event was over, everyone in their party had hit at least one bingo except Ralph and Gus. Ralph groused about it on the way home. "I must have missed by one number a dozen times," he said. "Guess it just wasn't my night."

"You can have my certificate for a free class at the center," Skye said. "I can't use it."

"Why not?" Belle asked. "They have lots of neat classes. I had a hard time choosing."

"Well, I have the clinic."

"How about Thursday morning?" Belle asked. "I'm taking a yoga class then. It's only an hour. Go with me. It will be fun."

Skye hesitated, glancing at her mother, who sat beside her. "I'll think about it."

"Great," Belle said. "Do you know where to buy a yoga mat?"

"I do," Flora said. "There's a shop just down from Daisy's

Health Food Store that carries them. And they have really cute workout clothes, golf togs and such. Winnie Satterwhite buys things there all the time."

"I'll check it out tomorrow."

When they reached home, everyone scattered except Belle and Gabe.

Gabe set the lamp he carried—one of the prizes Belle had won—on the hall table. "Want a nightcap?"

"What did you have in mind?"

"I can offer wine or hot chocolate."

"Hot chocolate sounds great."

"Are you going to keep that?" He nodded to the lamp with its Tiffany-style stained-glass shade.

"Of course I am. I plan to use it in my new place."

Gabe put his hand to her back to guide her toward the kitchen and the tingles started zipping again.

"Where is your new place going to be?"

"I haven't decided yet. I suppose that will depend on my career decisions."

"Wimberley could always use another lawyer."

Belle shuddered. "Not for me. I'd like to avoid anything having to do with law, law enforcement, or any level of the government."

Gabe heated milk in the microwave while Belle got mugs from the cabinet. "If real estate interests you, you could have a place at my agency. Of course it takes some training."

"Thanks. I don't mind the training, but that doesn't seem right to me, either. I want to do something a little more... different. That's vague, I know, but it's the best I can do." She dumped a packet of mix into each mug. "I want to be able to express some inner part of myself. Does that sound goofy?"

He grinned. "You're asking my mother's son if something sounds goofy?"

She laughed. "She's not goofy. She's gifted. I wish I could paint like she does. Or make pottery like your stepfather."

"You're taking ceramics now. Maybe you'll find that it's your forte."

"Sure," she said. "My talents with clay aren't any better than my drawings. You thought the coil pot I made today was something the dog deposited."

"Oh, come on, Belle. It wasn't that bad."

"Granted that it looked a little better before Alma stepped on it, but not too much."

He chuckled. "At least you have a sense of humor."

"A sense of humor came with the Outlaw name. My whole family is a bunch of jokers. Maybe I should consider stand-up comedy."

He poured hot water into their mugs and handed her a spoon. "When is your divorce final?"

"Is that a not-so-subtle change of subject?"

"Not at all. I was just wondering."

She started to ask him why he'd been wondering, but didn't. "I'm expecting the papers in the next few days. I'm having them mailed to one of my sisters-in-law's office. She's an attorney, and I figured that she'd keep quiet about it until I can properly break the news to my parents. Which reminds me, I need to call Carrie and alert her."

"That soon?"

"What soon?"

"Your divorce."

"Neither of us were interested in dragging things out. It was uncontested and uncomplicated by property or children, so the judge expedited things. And Matt's in a hurry to marry his pregnant fiancée."

"Bitter?"

"Of course." She leaned against the kitchen island and sipped her drink. "Well, less bitter than humiliated I suppose. The whole experience has left me feeling…undesirable."

"That's nuts." He plucked the mug from her hands, set it aside and drew her close to him, locking his arms around her waist. "Lady, you are prodigiously desirable."

"I am?"

"Yes," he said, brushing his lips across her forehead, "you are."

His mouth moved from forehead to eyelids to lips. There was nothing tentative about his kiss. It was warm and moist and urgent. She meant to push him away. Push him away and discuss boundaries and intentions. But her brain turned to Swiss cheese. She kissed him back with a fervor that rocked her.

Finally, she pulled back, gasping for air. "Was that a mercy kiss?"

"A mercy kiss?"

"Yes, you know, sort of like a mercy—"

He kissed her again to cut off her words. His mouth didn't feel merciful. It felt like a take-no-prisoners attack. And she did nothing to resist. His lips felt too good.

And his hands, which had crept under her shirt to cup her breasts, felt too good.

And his hardness pressing against her felt too good.

"Come with me," Gabe said, his voice hoarse.

"Where?"

"To my rooms."

She considered it, considered it seriously. "I—I can't, Gabe. It's too soon for me. Please understand."

He sighed and leaned his forehead against hers. "I do understand. Sorry I pushed, but you're so damned desirable that I think about you all the time. That Matt character is a fruitcake. Don't let his stupidity do a number on you." He stepped away, picked up her mug and handed it to her.

She took a sip. "It's cooled off."

"I can warm it up in nothing flat." He lifted an eyebrow.

Belle laughed in spite of her efforts not to. "Gabe, you're very good for my ego."

"And you're very good for my libido."

"I think I'd better call it a night."

"Okay. But remember, the invitation is open anytime you feel ready."

"Should I say *thanks*?"

He smiled. "*Yes* would be better."

GABE FELT LIKE A LOUSE pushing Belle, but he wanted her in the worst way. If Sam Outlaw could read Gabe's mind at that moment, he'd probably kill him. He hadn't set out to fall for her, hadn't intended to spend a good part of his nights tossing and turning just knowing that she was in bed upstairs in his house. Maybe it was the womanly way that her hips swayed when she walked or the cute way that a dimple appeared in one cheek when she smiled that had gotten under his skin. Or maybe it was the way she smelled or held her cup. Maybe it was the warm way she had with Flora and Skye and Suki and everybody else—even the animals. Whatever it was, something had knocked the props out from under him.

Gabe tried to tell himself to back off. She needed a friend, not a lover, he reminded himself over and over. What could he offer Belle in any case? She deserved a man who could make a total commitment to her—and he couldn't. His priority must always be his family—his mother and his sister. He couldn't let them down again and live with himself. They needed him, and he had to be willing to make whatever sacrifice he must to keep them safe and happy.

Over and over he told himself that and struggled with it. But, God help him, he would see Belle, catch his reflection in those tantalizing eyes, hear her laugh, and he'd be lost. All he could think of was touching her, holding her close and loving her.

He couldn't have it all, but damn, he wanted it. How could he give her up when she had become as important to him as breathing?

Maybe she could understand his commitment and live with it. She was different from Lisa. Wasn't she? Or were there things that all women wanted and deserved that he couldn't provide? He could only hope that maybe life could work out for them, somehow, sometime in the future. When she was ready. He couldn't let her go.

He would wait. And hope.

BELLE CONSIDERED DELAYING going downstairs the following morning. This thing between Gabe and her was becoming awkward, particularly with others in the household. But she longed for coffee, so she pulled on her bathing suit, the one-piece she had left, and her sweats over that, then went in search of caffeine.

She needn't have been concerned. Gabe had already left for an early appointment and only Skye was at the table finishing her breakfast.

"Anything special planned for today?" Skye asked.

"After a swim, I'm going in search of a yoga mat. May I get one for you? I'd love to have you join me."

Skye hesitated.

Rather than wait for an excuse, Belle plowed on. "Skye, I don't mean to interfere in your business, but it's obvious that you have security issues. Trust me, you'll be safe with me. I have a black belt in karate, and I'll even take my gun along. I won't let anything happen to you. We can have Ralph or one of the guards drive us there if that will help."

Skye hesitated again, then Belle could see a subtle shift in her expression. "Okay. I'll do it."

Belle smiled. "Great! I'll get a yoga mat for you, too. Thursday morning at nine-thirty, we'll learn to be pretzels."

Skye laughed. "I hope I don't dislocate anything."

After Skye left for the clinic, Belle did a few laps in the pool, then dressed and drove to town searching for the shop Flora had mentioned.

The place wasn't hard to find, and she bought non-slip mats as well as two pairs of yoga pants that were on sale, one for her and one for Skye. A boutique next door was also having a sale, and Belle wandered in, always ready for a bargain. She found a good deal on a couple of skirts and tops that were dressier than the clothes she had with her. She even found a cute pair of shoes in her size at a sale price.

After she dumped her purchases in the backseat, she wandered around town, going inside a few places that interested her, and ended up at the Firefly, the gallery that sold Flora's things.

"Good morning," Mason, the proprietor, said. "Where's Flora?"

"She's at home working on those commissions that you twisted her arm to do."

He laughed. "She always fusses, but she loves it. Has she finished your portrait yet?"

"Not yet. She had to put it aside temporarily. How did you know she was doing mine?"

"I know Flora. You're very interesting, and she can't resist. I'm about to close shop for lunch. Will you join me?"

"Oh, dear. Is it lunchtime already?" She checked her watch, then discovered it was missing. "I forgot my watch."

"You must be settling into Wimberley time."

"That has to be like Naconiche time. My oldest brother swears that when you move there, time slows down and your blood pressure drops twenty points."

Mason smiled. "Same phenomenon here. Come have lunch with me. It's not every day I have a chance to escort a beautiful woman."

"How can I resist such an offer? Let me call and tell everyone where I am."

After Belle made the call, she and Mason walked across the street to a neat sandwich shop with an old-fashioned grill turning out hamburgers that smelled heavenly. She hadn't had a hamburger in ages and ordered one. They got drinks and found a table outside on the patio.

"So," Mason said, "are you enjoying Wimberley?"

"Very much so. I'm falling in love with the place. It's a delightful town."

"It is. I'll be sad to leave."

"You're leaving? Flora didn't mention it."

"It's a recent decision and I've only just told her. My partner's mother lives in Dallas, and she's quite ill. He's her only child, and he feels obligated to move closer to her so that he can supervise her care properly."

"She can't move here?"

Mason shook his head. "We've explored that option. Leaving her home and friends would be very traumatic for her, and she needs the specialized care found in a city. He's moving this week, and, as soon as I can find a buyer for the gallery, I'll be moving as well. Know anybody who might be interested?"

Belle was about to say no when a sudden thought struck. She was looking for a new career. Maybe this was an option. Gallery owner.

Hmm. Something to consider. If she couldn't paint or sculpt, she could at least rub elbows with artists if she had a gallery.

"Possibly," she said. "Let me give it some thought. What's involved?"

He told her a bit about the day-to-day operations of the Firefly, and it didn't seem too complicated. She wasn't confident about her eye for the right pieces, but no doubt Flora could help her with that.

The more she thought about it, the more excited she became, but she didn't mention her ideas to Mason. Not yet.

She needed to talk with Gabe and Flora before making such a serious commitment.

Their sandwiches came, and they chatted while they ate. She really liked him. A shame that his going might make a place for her.

After thanking him for lunch, they parted, and Belle made it back to Gabe's in time to have coffee with the family. Napoleon was still eating.

"Did you buy out the stores?" Gabe asked.

"Not quite. But I bought yoga mats and pants for Skye and me."

Gabe glanced at Skye, then back to Belle. "Yoga mats and pants?"

"Yes. I have a friend who always said that half the battle of learning to play tennis was first buying a really cute outfit. Bev never did learn to play tennis very well, but she was voted the best-dressed person at the club."

Skye and Flora chuckled, but Gabe only look confused. "You and Skye are going to learn yoga?"

"Yes. On Thursday mornings at the center."

Gabe broke into a grin. "Great. That's great. I'll drive you. What time is your class?"

"Nine-thirty," Belle said. "But it's not necessary for you to drive us. I'll drive."

Gabe glanced again at Skye, who nodded. "Okay then. But I'm available if you change your mind."

"Thanks, but I think we'll be okay," Skye said.

"I'm taking my gun," Belle said.

"Oh, good heavens!" Flora said, looking alarmed.

"Mo-ther," Skye said. "She's an ex-FBI agent and an expert marksman."

"Oh, yes. I forgot. Have you actually ever shot anyone?"

"Not lately," Belle said. "Not since I was five and shot my brother J.J. in the foot with an air rifle."

Flora tittered. "I'll wager he never lets you forget it."

"Never. Flora, are you sure that you won't join us?"

"I'll leave that to you young people." Flora pushed away from the table and stood. "Now, I have to get back to my studio and work on these paintings that Mason insisted I take. Excuse me, please."

"I have something I'd like to talk with you about later," Belle said. "When you take a break."

"Mother forgets to take breaks," Gabe said.

"That's true. I'm guilty. Why don't you drop in mid-afternoon with a glass of iced tea or lemonade?"

"Will do."

"What in tarnation is yoga pants?" Suki asked as she scurried around picking up dishes.

"Well," Belle said, "they're sort of like sweatpants, only shorter and lighter weight. Skye, you probably should try yours for fit. I guessed at the size."

"I'll do that tonight. Thanks for picking up the mat and pants. Tell me how much they were, and I'll pay you for them."

"No you won't. Consider them a hostess gift. You've all done so much for me that it's the least I can do."

"Thank you, Belle. We love having you here, don't we, Gabe?"

"Absolutely."

Napoleon was finishing off a piece of pie when Skye said,

"We'd better get a move on, Napoleon. Jim Bledsoe should be delivering those lambs any minute."

"What lambs?" Gabe asked. "Are we getting lambs?"

"Only two," Skye said. "They're to give Carlotta something to do and keep her from being lonely and getting into trouble."

"What is she supposed to do with the lambs?"

"Supervise them."

Gabe laughed. "That'll be the day."

"Actually, llamas are frequently used like shepherds," Skye said. "With a bit of training, I'm sure she'll do great."

"I hope Carlotta doesn't teach the lambs to ring the doorbell," Suki said. "Anybody want any more coffee?"

"Not me," Belle said, and the others declined as well.

Napoleon, Skye and Gus left, and Suki bustled off to her chores, leaving Belle and Gabe alone at the sunroom table.

"Sounds like you've had a busy day so far," Gabe said.

"I have, and there's something that I'd like to discuss with you as well."

"Nothing ominous, I hope."

Belle realized that she was frowning and relaxed. "No, just something I'm considering. Mason is selling his gallery, and I'm considering buying it. Does that seem crazy to you?"

"I think that it's a fabulous idea."

"You said that too quickly," Belle said. "I think you're supposed to consider profit-and-loss statements or something."

Gabe grinned. "I know that Mason earns enough from the gallery to make a decent living. His products are all consignment, so the inventory doesn't cost him anything. His only overhead is his lease and utilities. I own the building, so I could cut you a deal on it. I'll even sponsor you in the merchant's association. Anything that will keep you here permanently is a fantastic idea. Need financing? I'm your man."

She laughed. "Whoa, fellow. It's just an option that I'm considering, not a done deal. I'd need to investigate more. A lot more."

"I vote yes," he said. And kissed her.

Chapter Twelve

Flora voted yes, too. "It will be awful losing Mason, but it will be wonderful gaining you. I'll help in any way I can, but I'm sure the artists that show at the Firefly now will be delighted to continue with you."

"It's still only an avenue to explore," Belle said. "I might find that I hate owning a gallery. And that would be terrible."

"You're right. It would be nice if you could try it on like trying on a pair of shoes," Flora said. "I know! Why don't you spend a day or two at the gallery and get a feel for it. Do you feel up to doing that?"

"Of course. Great idea. I'll talk to Mason tomorrow. In the meantime, please don't mention it to anyone, Flora."

"My lips are sealed."

"I'll let you get back to work then. I have an appointment with Sally for a haircut in a few minutes."

"Oh, but your hair is so beautiful. I hope you're not going to get one of those short, scruffy things that looks as if it needs a good brushing. Not that it's any of my concern, of course."

Belle smiled. "I'm just getting a trim. I like to keep it long enough to put up when I don't have time to mess with it. See you later."

A few minutes later she parked in front of Sally's hair salon, which was across the street and down a bit from the Firefly.

When she went inside, Sally fluttered her fingers. "Hi, Belle. I'm running about twenty minutes behind. Do you have a quick errand?"

"Sure," Belle said. "I'll go do a bit of window-shopping."

Outside, she glanced across at the Firefly, then decided to talk to Mason until Sally was ready for her.

He was alone in the gallery.

"Well, hello," he said, looking up from a magazine and smiling. "I wasn't expecting to see you again today."

"I'm waiting my turn for a haircut from Sally, and I wanted to talk with you about something."

"About buying the gallery?"

"Boy, that was faster than a speeding bullet. Have you talked to Flora?"

"No. Bea McClure mentioned that you might be interested."

"I don't even know Bea McClure."

"She's with Gabe's real estate agency," Mason said.

Belle frowned. "Gabe has a big mouth."

"Don't be upset with him. I talked with Bea about listing both my house and the business. That's how that came about."

"Oh. Good to know. Listen, Mason, I know nothing about running a gallery, and I might not be cut out for the business. I was wondering if I could hang out a couple of days and get a feel for things."

"Sure. Anytime."

They decided on Friday and Saturday as the best days for her to come in. "Saturday will be wild, and I could use the help."

"What's happening on Saturday?"

"This will be the first Market Day of the season."

"Market Day?"

"It's a zoo. On the first Saturday of the month, there are four hundred and fifty booths in an area just down the road, and Wimberley has lots of visitors. It's more a bazaar than flea market, and vendors sell everything from windmills to wind chimes. Be prepared."

"I'll see you on Friday at ten. Do you have a dress code?"

"Shoes if you feel like it."

Belle laughed. "It ain't New York."

"It ain't."

When she got back to the hair salon, Sally was waiting. "I understand you may buy the Firefly and stay in Wimberley."

"Holy moly! Has Bea McClure been here?"

"Not today. Do you know Bea?"

"Never met her, but for the record, I have no definite plans to buy the Firefly. I'm only considering it as a possibility."

"I'll update my source. I hope you do decide to buy a business and stay. I have a feeling we could be great friends. Now, do you want color or just a cut?"

FORTY-FIVE MINUTES LATER, Belle walked out of Sally's salon feeling great. Her haircut was perfect, and she felt as if she'd made a new friend. The two of them had talked nonstop for the entire time. And it seemed that Sally was enrolled in the Thursday yoga class as well.

"I don't work on Thursdays," Sally had said. "It's my running-around day."

She found herself singing as she drove home. Well, not home exactly, but to Gabe's house. She felt better than she had any day since Matt had dropped his bombshell on her. Looked like she'd survived that ordeal and come through without major scars.

Her cell phone rang just after she passed through the guard post. Her sister-in-law Carrie told her that her divorce papers had been delivered to her office in the afternoon mail.

"Hallelujah!" Belle said. "I'm a free woman."

"Going to go out and celebrate?" Carrie asked.

"Not exactly. I'm going to a creative writing class tonight."

"Sounds…interesting."

"It's part of my effort to keep busy. You haven't told anyone about the divorce, have you?"

"No, not even Frank, and that's been hard. Don't worry. I'll keep quiet. When are you coming home? Everybody is eager to see you."

"Not for a couple of weeks. I figured I'd stay until the doctor releases me."

"We have doctors in Naconiche," Carrie said. "As I recall, our sister-in-law happens to be quite good." Dr. Kelly Martin Outlaw was not only married to Cole, the oldest Outlaw brother, but she was Carrie's dear friend and an excellent physician.

"I know, but I'm going to hang around here for a while. How are Frank and the twins?"

"Fabulous. And both Mary Beth and I are getting big as barrels. It's a shame you have to be pregnant to have babies. If it had been left up to me, I'd have found a less cumbersome way." Carrie caught her up on all the family gossip.

Belle sat in the garage and listened, then hung up just as Gabe pulled into the slot beside her. She waved, and they got out of their vehicles at the same time.

"I like your hair," he said, touching it.

"Thanks. Sally just cut it."

"I know."

"Lord, did the *Star* put out a special bulletin today? It seems as if everybody in Wimberley knows my business. Bea McClure had already told Mason my intentions before I could talk to him, and I've never even said boo to the woman."

Gabe laughed. "My fault. Bea told me that Mason had listed his business and house with her, and I simply mentioned that I might know someone who was interested in the gallery. All very innocent, I promise."

"Then how did Sally find out about it?"

"My secretary must have mentioned it. I think Martha was Sally's appointment just before you. Sorry. I'll tell her to put a cork in it." He pulled her into his arms. "But you know how small towns are. There are no secrets."

"I know. But I hate for information to get out about something that's only a possibility." She told Gabe about her plans to spend Friday and Saturday at the Firefly.

"Are you sure you're up to it?"

"I'm sure."

"Want to go for a ride before dinner? I can tell Manuel to saddle the horses for us."

"I'd love it. Let me change."

THE DAY HAD BEEN just about perfect, Belle thought as she and Gabe walked back to the house after their ride. He had taken her hand casually as they strolled along, and it felt very right. Very natural.

"I hope this situation with the gallery works out," Gabe said.

"It almost seems too easy, but I've always been a skeptic about things falling into my lap."

"Then I won't give you Flora's adage about your path finding you if you keep walking and don't worry too much about it."

Belle smiled. "Sounds like Flora, but it's very hard to change habits when all your life you've been a goal-oriented pragmatist."

"I know. I fall into that category myself. Want to drive over to San Marcos and see a movie tonight?"

"Sorry, but tonight is my creative writing class."

"Oh, that's right. I hope you enjoy it."

Belle had never enjoyed anything less. After dinner she'd driven to the center with great anticipation. There had been only five people in her class, including Steve, the veteran from her ceramics group. It became abundantly clear early on that she wasn't cut out for creative writing. The instructor had given them a quick writing exercise to do, and then everybody read theirs. Steve's was fabulous. Even the elderly woman who was writing her memoir penned a page that was very interesting.

Hers had sucked swamp water. It sounded more like a case report than anything creative. And her sentences were little better than "See Spot run and play." She'd been humiliated.

Oh, everyone had been very polite, but it was obvious that she had no flair for prose. Loving to read didn't translate to talent for writing. She would have chucked the whole endeavor that night if Steve hadn't talked her out of it.

"Give it some time," he'd said as they'd left after class.

"You have a fascinating background. I'll bet you could come up with a great plot for a mystery."

Belle didn't hold out much hope, but she hated being a quitter. That's why she'd stuck with the FBI as long as she had.

She'd gone directly to her rooms and soaked in a bubble bath for an hour. Bubble baths were always more soothing than a shot of bourbon.

She'd just pulled on her nightshirt when she heard a tapping on her door. It was Skye.

"I just wanted to see if you're okay," she said.

"I'm fine," Belle told her. "Just a little tired from a busy day. Thanks for asking."

Skye hesitated as if she wanted to talk more, then said, "You'll want to make an early night of it then."

"I think so. I'll see you at breakfast."

Skye smiled, and she and Gus continued down the hall to her suite.

Belle had barely picked up her book when someone knocked on the door again. This time it was Flora.

"Are you all right, dear?" Flora asked.

"Fine, thanks. Just a little tired."

"Have you given any more thought to buying the Firefly?"

"Some, but my mind was occupied with the class tonight."

"How did that go?"

"Let's put it this way—Mary Higgins Clark has nothing to fear from me."

Flora laughed. "I can barely write a coherent letter myself. But the important thing is to enjoy yourself and open yourself to a variety of experiences. I always say that if you keep walking, your path will find you."

"I certainly hope so."

"Well, good night, dear."

"Good night, Flora."

Belle hoped that nobody else came knocking. That was the bad thing about being in a large household. Privacy was always an issue.

She had barely formed the thought when there was another knock. Probably Gabe this time.

Scowling, she flung open the door.

But instead of Gabe, Suki stood there with a bowl.

"Something wrong?" Suki asked.

"No," Belle said. "I thought you might be Gabe."

"Nope. He went to a meeting of some kind, but it looks like he's got his tail in a crack."

"Really?"

Suki grinned. "You looked like you could chew barbed wire when you opened that door."

"Oh, sorry. My mind was somewhere else."

"I understand that. I fixed some homemade ice cream after you left, and I thought you might like some."

"Thanks, Suki. I love ice cream, especially homemade."

"Gabe said you did. You'd better get to eating it afore it melts."

"I will. It's very sweet of you to bring it to me. I hate to be extra trouble."

"You're no trouble. Glad to do it. It's been good having you around here. Seems like everybody is a little happier since you've been here. You're not like some other folks I could name. And that's good. Well, I'll quit running off at the mouth and get on. See you in the morning."

After Suki left, Belle looked down at the ice cream and felt guilty and ungrateful. Everyone in the household had been supernice to her and here she was bitching about privacy.

And the ice cream was great.

THE CERAMICS CLASS was a hoot. The glazing part of the lesson went okay. Everybody had painted their pinch pots and boxes for firing in the kiln without any major glitches. But learning to use the potter's wheel was another story. It wasn't as easy as Molly, their instructor, made it look. Thank goodness for old clothes because they slung wet clay everywhere, and Belle's first attempt at forming a bowl looked like a lopsided fortune cookie.

The good thing was that she didn't feel too bad since nobody produced anything that looked much better. They'd all had a good laugh, and she, Steve and the twin sisters went out to lunch again. This time they had spaghetti at the Methodist church for some fund-raising event. The food was quite good, and the Culbertsons introduced Belle to so many people that she couldn't remember all their names. Several had already heard that she was buying the Firefly, and she had to explain that was a premature rumor.

"Want to come to the shooting range with us tonight?" Alma asked as they were about to split up.

"I think I will," Belle said. "What time?"

They settled on a time and Thelma gave her directions to the place.

"Ladies shoot free on Wednesday nights," Alma reminded her, "but they have to buy their ammunition from Red. I guess that's only fair."

On the way home Belle laughed at herself for palling around with a pair of old-maid school teachers who were older than her mother, but she really enjoyed them. And she liked Steve as well. He'd planned on going into law enforcement after his hitch in the Marines was up, but the bomb had ended those dreams. He was starting back to college in the fall—majoring in what, he didn't know. Sounded like her. Neither of them knew what they were going to do with the rest of their lives. He'd checked into vocational counseling for a start. Didn't sound like a half-bad idea. Maybe she ought to consider it.

BELLE HAD A GREAT TIME shooting with Alma and Thelma Culbertson. Both the old gals were pretty good shots.

When she got home that night, she found Gabe sitting in the shadows on the front porch.

"Well, hello there," she said.

"Hello, yourself. You're getting to be such a gadabout that I haven't seen much of you."

"I saw you at dinner."

"But that was with the whole tribe. Want to join me in a glass of wine?"

She noticed a bottle and two glasses on the table beside his rocker. "Sure." She sat down in the other chair while he poured.

"How did your evening with the Culbertsons go?"

"Very well." She sipped from her glass.

Gabe chuckled. "Somehow I still can't imagine those two packing Glocks."

"A Smith and Wesson, actually. They share it. And they're pretty darned good. Do you shoot?"

"Occasionally. Just enough to keep up my skills. I took a few lessons and got a concealed weapon permit just after Skye…had her ordeal."

Again she waited for him to elaborate. He didn't. "I didn't realize that you carried a gun."

"I usually keep one in the glove compartment of the car. Can I top that off for you?" He motioned to her glass with the bottle.

"I'm fine. One is my limit tonight or I'll never get up in the morning. Tomorrow is when Skye and I go to yoga class."

"I know. She's nervous. But I'm very pleased that she's going with you. Thanks for encouraging her."

"No problem. I like Skye."

"She likes you, too. Rather she's in awe of you."

Belle laughed. "In *awe* of me?"

"Of your courage."

"I'm not particularly courageous. True, I'm not afraid of much, but not being afraid isn't the same thing as having courage."

"It isn't?"

She shook her head. "I don't think so." She yawned. "Sorry. It's not the company. I'm fading fast. It's been a busy day. I don't need naps anymore, but I run out of steam early."

"Come on," Gabe said, pulling her to her feet. "I'll walk you to your door. Take your glass."

He put his hand to her back as they walked upstairs, and that slithery feeling started again. She'd wanted to mention that she'd received her final divorce papers, but she couldn't figure out how to work it into the conversation.

When they reached her door, Gabe took the glass from her

fingers with one hand and lifted her chin with the other. "How about a date Friday night?"

"A date?"

"Uh-huh. Do you like to dance?"

"Love it."

"They have live music at one of the places downtown on Friday and Saturday nights. Texas swing this weekend I believe."

"Ahh-hah," she sang. "San Antone."

He laughed. "I see you're familiar with Texas swing."

"Naturally. I'm a Texan. East Texan at that."

"There are some Texans who don't know a thing about country-and-western dancing."

She thought of his ex-fiancée. "I'm not one of them. I love country-and-western dancing. I love any kind of dancing. What I lack in skill, I make up in enthusiasm."

He kissed her briefly. "You're such a pleasure. We'll have fun."

"Count on it."

He kissed her again. This time his tongue teased hers, and his lips became more insistent.

She wrapped her arms around him and kissed him back with a matching insistence.

"Belle, dear, I—"

Flora's voice came from the stairs, and Belle quickly pushed away.

"Oops," Flora said. "Sorry. Don't mind me. Just keep doing what you were doing."

Too late. The moment was lost. Belle said good night and slipped inside the door.

THERE WERE A FEW TIMES when Gabe wanted to throttle his mother. This was one of them. But his life was not his own, and he reminded himself of that commitment he'd made. His mother and sister were his primary concern. Always. Sometimes it was hard. Especially when someone as exceptional as Belle had come into his life.

He sighed and went downstairs.

Chapter Thirteen

Skye didn't say anything, but Belle could tell that she was a little nervous when they picked up their yoga mats and headed for the car. Except for Gus being along, they could have been two ordinary girlfriends out for the morning.

They arrived ten minutes early for the Thursday morning class, and Sally showed up a minute later. In fact, Skye knew all of the ten women and the one man who made up the class, as well as the instructor, which wasn't unusual since she'd grown up in Wimberley and also treated most of their pets. Belle recognized only Sally, Katie, the young mother from ceramics class, and Roger, the retired colonel from that same class.

They spent the hour learning to deep breathe properly and do a few simple poses for stretching and balance.

"I already love this stuff," Sally said after the class.

"Me, too," Skye said. "I can't believe I haven't tried it until now."

"I don't feel at all like a pretzel," Belle said and every-body laughed.

"Do y'all have time for a cup of coffee?" Sally asked.

Belle glanced at Skye, who hesitated, then said, "Sure. Why not."

Surprised by Skye's response, Belle quickly agreed, and they followed Sally's car to a coffee shop on the square. The proprietor didn't seem to mind Gus tagging along, and the three women had a terrific time talking and laughing.

Skye glanced at her watch. "Oh, my, look at the time. Gabe will think we've stood him up."

"Why don't you call him and have him meet us at the restaurant?" Belle said. "We can hang around here or do some shopping. That little boutique down the street is having a fabulous sale."

"Maybe next time," Skye said. "I'd like to shower and change."

"Sounds like a good idea."

They said goodbye to Sally and drove back home. Skye simply glowed. "That was so much fun," she said. "I really enjoyed myself, Belle. Thanks for suggesting the class."

"My pleasure. And I didn't have to shoot a soul."

Skye laughed.

BY NOON ON FRIDAY, Belle was wondering whatever gave her the idea that she wanted to buy the Firefly. They hadn't had a single customer and only a couple of lookers. Oh, she and Mason enjoyed talking, but if business was usually this slow, she'd be bored out of her gourd. Mason assured her that weekends were brisker, but, even if that were true, what was she going to do the rest of the week? And did she really want to work weekends?

By four o'clock, after a yawner of a day, Belle decided to pack it in.

"Things will pick up tomorrow," Mason said.

She certainly hoped so.

After practicing her yoga for half an hour, Belle took a long bath and dressed in her best jeans and boots for her date with Gabe. She wondered if the date really were a date or if half the household were going along.

Looked as if it really was a date. After dinner, Gabe escorted her out to his car, and they drove to downtown Wimberley—which took three and a half minutes driving slowly.

"Where did all the cars come from?" Belle asked when they reached the square.

"From out of the hills and hollers. Lots of folks are here for the music and dancing tonight. Others are vendors in town for Market Day tomorrow. Gates open at six in the morning. This place looks like an anthill on first Saturday. The Lions Club runs the event, but half the town pitches in. I'll be down working first thing."

"Are you a Lion?"

"Yes, ma'am." He roared, then they laughed.

They finally found a parking place in an alley and walked toward the dance hall behind the restaurant. She could hear the notes of a fiddle sawing through the cool night air and heard an occasional "Yee-haw!" mixed with the guitar and bass.

"Sounds like the party has already started," Belle said.

"It's just getting warmed up. There'll be plenty left for us." He put his arm around her waist as they walked, and the heady scent of his aftershave sent a thrill through her.

There were still a couple of tables available near the dance floor, and they grabbed one. Gabe held up two fingers to the waiter, who soon brought a pair of long-necks and a basket of unshelled peanuts.

"Want to take a spin?" he asked.

"You betcha," Belle said, jumping up. "Are you going to insist on leading?"

He laughed. "We can take turns."

Gabe was a great two-stepper with a strong lead, so she deferred to him. Matt had been only so-so and half the time she'd had to drag him around the floor. Gabe even swung her out with a little fancy footwork, and she had a blast.

The next song was a waltz, and his lead was strong and his movements graceful. They stopped after that one and sipped from their beers. Belle had never cared much for beer, but the peanuts seemed to make it better.

She spotted Sally in the crowd and waved. Sally came over pulling a tall, slim man behind her and introduced him as Tim, her husband who owned one of the local wineries. Gabe, of course, already knew both of them.

They danced and laughed and hooted and had a general blast until Belle felt herself beginning to grow tired.

Gabe must have noticed because he leaned close and said, "Are you about ready to leave?"

"No. I want to dance until dawn, but my body is rebelling. Let's have two more dances."

After three more, they waved to the group sitting around them and left. Belle's feet were still doing a shuffle all the way to the car. "I loved this."

"I'm glad," Gabe said, swinging her out and twirling her around at the car door. "I had fun, too. I haven't been dancing in quite a while."

"You're very good."

"Thanks." He grinned and bumped her hip with his. "I noticed that you didn't try to lead much."

"*Much?* I didn't lead at all, Gabe Burrell. I didn't have to, but, believe me, I'm not above leading when I have to."

"I hope your ex-husband was a lousy dancer."

"He was."

"Good." He opened the door and helped her into the car. "I want to be better at everything than he was." He leaned down and kissed her, then closed the door.

She had a feeling he would be. She already knew that he was a better dancer and a better kisser.

ON SATURDAY MORNING, Belle couldn't believe the amount of traffic that had invaded one very small town. Thank heavens that Ralph insisted on driving her to the gallery. She would have never found a parking place. Suki had told her that Gabe had left before breakfast to be at his post for the day, but not to worry. There was lots of food on the grounds, she'd said.

While the Market Day booths were on a tract of land a short distance from the square, a mob of people were there as well. Spillover to local merchants was one of the advantages.

"Good morning," Mason said when she went in the door.

"Hope I'm not late."

"Not at all. I just opened."

The gallery was much busier on Saturday than it had been the day before. Lots of folks trekked through the gallery, mostly lookers, but others were serious customers. Everyone fell in love with Flora's soul paintings, and Belle soon had her spiel about them down pat. By mid-afternoon, they'd sold five paintings, three of them bluebonnet landscapes, and had deposits for three commissions for Flora.

"Are weekends always this brisk?" Belle asked when they had a breather.

"No. Market Day makes a difference, but weekends are busier than weekdays, and there's a seasonal surge as well."

"Christmas?"

"Always good for business."

A jingle at the door signaled another customer, but Belle turned to find Gabe there in a bright blue T-shirt and an equally bright yellow ball cap.

"How's business?" he asked.

"Not bad. How are things at the market?" she asked.

"On a glorious day like today and opening of the season? It's wall-to-wall people. Want to play hooky for a while and walk around the grounds?"

Belle glanced at Mason. "Go ahead," he said. "Market Day should be experienced. Take cash."

"What's this?" Belle asked when he led her to a golf cart double-parked outside.

"The only way to go. I confiscated it from a friend. Hop on."

She did and he drove with the creep-along traffic to the field a short distance away.

Belle saw everything from musicians to glass blowers, and she snacked on a corn dog as they walked through the rows of booths and checked out all the wares. Some peddled antiques, others handmade furniture, still others craft items and baked goods. She fell in love with the beautifully made wind chimes.

"I have to have one for myself, but they'll make perfect Christmas gifts for my married brothers and their wives."

"Christmas? But it's only April."

"I like to plan ahead."

She had a hard time selecting only four. The vendor, who was also the artist, boxed them for her, and Gabe carried the package as they explored other booths. She found an exquisite beaded eyeglass case for her mother and a great hand-tooled belt for her dad.

"At this rate, I'll have all my shopping done by the end of the day. Except for the kids. They always prefer toys. Say, this place is so terrific. And the prices are reasonable. Oh, would you look!" She hurried to the booth to look closely at a framed pen-and-ink drawing. "It's perfect for Sam, Gabe. Isn't it perfect?"

He looked closely at the cartoon drawing of an old cowboy on his horse, a Texas Ranger badge pinned to his shirt.

"Perfect, I'd say."

When the picture, which framed out at about twelve by fourteen, was purchased and wrapped, Belle put it on top of the packages Gabe already carried.

"I think we're going to have to leave," Belle said, "while you can still see over the top of the stack."

"No problem. I'll pay one of the volunteers to stash the stuff in the trunk of my car."

"Can you do that?"

"Sure," Gabe said. "Toting purchases is a big money-raiser. And it encourages people to buy more."

"I'm running out of cash, so I guess I'd better stop for the day."

"I'll loan you whatever you need."

Belle shook her head. "I'm on sensory overload already. There's so much to see and choose from. Oh, look, Gabe."

She grabbed his arm. "Cotton candy. I haven't had any since I was a kid."

"Then let's get some for you." He held up one finger to the vendor and fished out his wallet. "My treat."

She watched the pink sugar being spun and wrapped on to a paper cone until it was a big fluffy ball. While Gabe was paying, she pulled a piece from the cone and let it melt in her mouth. Heavenly. She felt like a teenager again at the Naconiche County Fair.

"Getting tired?" Gabe asked.

"Not at all," she said, "but I'd better get back to the gallery."

She plucked another piece of cotton candy and held it to his mouth. He opened wide, and she stuffed the wad in.

He found a volunteer that he knew and gave him the packages and his car keys, then drove her back to the gallery on the golf cart that was stashed by the front gate. With Belle feeding him alternate bites, the two of them demolished the cotton candy on the way.

"I do love Wimberley," she said. "It seems as if there's always something going on."

"There is. We have the Butterfly Festival this month, and the bluebonnets will be in bloom. The local theater group has a play starting next week. And there's always bingo."

"And dancing."

"That, too," he said as he pulled to a stop outside the gallery. "What are the prospects of your buying the Firefly?"

"I'm still thinking about it, but I have some reservations. I'll talk to you about it later." She climbed from the cart. "Thanks for the tour."

"You're welcome. I'll see you tonight."

BELLE THOUGHT A LOT about buying the Firefly over the next couple of days. She and Mason had talked more on a quiet Monday afternoon, and they'd gone over his books. Mason taught a couple of art classes to supplement his income, plus he used slack time to paint in a corner of the gallery and sold his own paintings—an option not open to Belle.

In the long run, she decided that buying the gallery wasn't a good move for her financially. And she figured that all the downtime bored the heck out of her.

She hated to tell Mason, but, surprisingly, he agreed with her assessment. Flora was more disappointed. As was Gabe.

"It just wasn't right for me," Belle told him after dinner Monday night.

"I was hoping that it would be."

"Me, too. Can you imagine what it's like for me to be my age and not know what you want to be when you grow up? It's ridiculous. I feel so...so unfinished. And frustrated."

He pulled her up from their stargazing rock and into his arms. "The right thing will come along. Give it time."

She snuggled close, loving the smell of him and the cozy feel of his arms around her.

He kissed her then—a warm, lingering kiss that curled her toes and unfurled an aching deep inside. His tongue explored and tasted and plundered, and he groaned in pleasure. His hands slipped down to knead her bottom and pull her pelvis close against him.

He murmured her name, and she whimpered, drowning in sensation.

He wanted more, and so did she, but something inside made her pull away. She just wasn't ready for that level of intimacy. For once the lack of privacy in the house worked to her advantage. It stopped her cold. In the heat of the moment, she might have done something totally nuts and hopped into his bed, but she wasn't comfortable with going to his rooms or hers and having everyone knowing exactly what they were doing. Somebody was bound to see them, and things would be awkward for everybody. But mostly for her.

Flora might be a free spirit, but she was, after all, his mother, and Belle wasn't blasé enough to make love with a man she'd known so briefly in the same house with his mother. And his sister. And the housekeeper and her husband. And the dogs. And the cats.

She laid her head on his shoulder. "I can't, Gabe. I'm sorry. I'm really sorry."

"Don't be. I understand."

She pulled back and looked up at him. "Do you? I don't mean to be a tease."

"I know. You still need time to heal."

"Maybe so, but I need to find my way slowly and not jump into a relationship the first thing out of the chute. Maybe I'm old-fashioned, but I'm not into casual sex."

"I didn't think you were." He kissed her forehead. "How did your ceramics class go today?"

"Don't ask."

"That bad?"

"For starters, my vase collapsed."

Chapter Fourteen

On Wednesday, the same thing happened again. This time it was a pot that collapsed on the wheel instead of a vase. Not even her first week of FBI training at Quantico had been this hard. She was frustrated out of her mind. The only time she remembered feeling remotely the same was when she was in elementary school and trying to make a topographical map of South America with flour and salt. It had looked like a green-and-brown veal cutlet.

"Why is it that yours looks so good," she asked Steve, "and mine looks so bad?"

He laughed. "I wouldn't say mine looks exactly good."

"Well, at least it's upright. Mine lists. Badly. And where did all those lumps come from?"

"I think you're trying too hard."

"I've heard that all my life, and I don't believe there is such a thing as trying too hard."

"What seems to be the problem?" Molly, the ceramics instructor, asked.

"I can't seem to get the hang of it," Belle said.

"I think you're trying too hard," Molly said, and Belle

rolled her eyes at Steve. "Relax and don't fight it. Find a rhythm. And use a smidgen less water."

When Molly moved on to help someone else, Belle whispered, "What's a smidgen?"

"About a half a teaspoon," Steve replied with a straight face.

She laughed. "You wouldn't know a smidgen if it jumped up and bit you on the butt."

"Sure I would. My grandmother was always talking about adding a smidgen of salt or something."

Belle wadded her clay into a ball and reseated it on the wheel. "Is she still living?"

He shook his head. "She died while I was gone. My grandfather is still alive though. I live with him. He's nearly eighty and quite a character." Steve's smile spoke of his fondness for the man.

"What about your parents?"

Steve shrugged. "I don't remember much about my dad. He left before I started to school. My mother left me with my grandparents while she got on her feet. I guess she never did because she didn't come back for me. Last I heard she was living somewhere in Louisiana. I think she got involved with drugs."

"A shame. I'm sorry."

"It's okay. I don't think much about her. Hey, don't go at that like fighting fire. Relax a little. You've got to caress the clay like you'd handle a—" He stopped and grinned. "I was about to say a woman, but I guess that wouldn't apply."

"Not really."

"How about like a man?"

"Let's not go there. How about like a baby?"

"I think you need to be a little firmer than that. Maybe. I don't know anything about babies."

With Steve holding her hands and helping her form the clay spinning on the electric wheel, she managed to end up with something that vaguely resembled a pot by the end of class.

Belle, Steve and the Culbertsons had spaghetti at the church again, then she went to see Dr. Hamilton afterward. Her two weeks were up on Thursday, but she figured that a day early wouldn't matter, so she'd made a Wednesday appointment. She'd talked to her mom the night before, and her family was eager to see her. She really couldn't put off going to Naconiche much longer.

While she was in the waiting room, Belle picked up a copy of the *Wimberley Star*. She read it quickly, then glanced at the classifieds under Help Wanted. Nothing there interested her. She didn't want to be a dental hygienist, a driver for a sanitation company, an after-school caretaker for a four-year-old or a mechanic for heavy equipment. She wasn't qualified for any of them except maybe the sanitation truck driver, and she didn't have a commercial driver's license.

Her glance went to the rentals in the next column, and a listing for a town house caught her attention. That gave her an idea. If she was going to consider living in Wimberley permanently, she ought to have her own place while she explored her options. Of course Gabe would insist that she stay with them, but, frankly, she longed for some privacy, and, despite what they said, she was sure that her being there for an extended period was an imposition on their hospitality.

She made a note of the management company's phone number, planning to call after she saw the doctor. If the town house looked good, she might rent it. At least she would have her own place. The nurse called her name just as she slipped her notepad back into her bag.

After examining her and asking several questions, Dr. Hamilton said, "I think you're doing great. Your lungs are clear and everything seems back to normal. You might be a bit low on energy for a while yet, but simply rest when you're tired and don't push too hard. You should be fine."

"That's good to hear. I need to go see my family in Naconiche."

"Leaving Wimberley?"

"Only temporarily. I like it here very much."

"So do I. You know I almost went to Naconiche when I was trying to decide where to set up my practice after I left the city."

"Really? My sister-in-law is in practice there."

"That wouldn't be Kelly Martin, would it?"

"Kelly Martin Outlaw now. She married my oldest brother. You know her? What a small world."

"She interned under me in Houston. Give her my best, and I know that you'll be in good hands if you need medical attention while you're gone."

Once in the car, Belle phoned the management company and discovered that they were in the next building. A woman named Michelle invited her to come on by.

Michelle was a tall, lanky blonde about Belle's age who moved like a greyhound. Looked a little like one, too. But she was very helpful. She took Belle to see two town houses, one in Woodcreek and one within walking distance of the square. She loved them both. The one in Woodcreek had a fireplace, but it also required a year's lease. The other she could get on a shorter-term agreement, even month-to-month if she wanted it.

That decided it. Besides, what did she need with a fireplace in April? She and the agent went back to the office and signed the papers. As Belle was writing the check, she said, "Michelle, I don't want my leasing this place to get out just yet, so I would appreciate it if you kept it to yourself."

"Of course," Michelle said, smiling. "Gabe doesn't know yet?"

"How did—" Belle practically sputtered.

"Just about everybody in town knows about you, and my boyfriend and I saw you two out dancing at Fancy's the other night."

"Oh. Well, the short answer is no. *Nobody* knows about my plans."

"Gotcha. Mum's the word."

I'll bet, Belle thought. But she decided to give Michelle the benefit of the doubt. She wasn't ready to tell Gabe yet.

A relationship with Gabe might work out and it might not. Granted they'd spent a lot of time together, but knowing someone only two or three weeks wasn't much. But she *was* interested in getting to know him better and seeing what a few months would bring. She didn't know what the future might hold, but Wimberley seemed to be a good base of operations while she explored some alternatives. With her savings and her oil-lease money, she had the luxury of waiting a while for just the right thing. And if the company that had leased the Outlaw property struck oil in the spot where they were drilling, she would have a steady income for a long time. She'd have to check out the situation while she was in Naconiche.

AT THE DINNER TABLE that evening, Belle said, "I went to see Dr. Hamilton today, and she said that I was healthy as a horse."

"Why, dear, that's delightful news," Flora said.

"Isn't it? I want to thank all of you for being so wonderful to me during my recovery. And since I'm doing okay now, I think it's time I leave before I wear out my welcome. I'm well past the three-day limit for fish and visitors."

Gabe felt a moment of panic when Belle made her announcement. There was dead silence, and everybody glanced at him except Belle. He supposed he knew at some level that she would leave eventually, but he hadn't planned on it being so soon.

"You're welcome to stay here as long as you like," Gabe said. "We enjoy having you here."

"Oh, yes," Skye said. "Don't go. What about our yoga class?"

"We'll go tomorrow," Belle said, "and I'll be back in town long before next Thursday. I'm only planning a long weekend in Naconiche with my family."

Gabe felt his heart start again. "You *are* coming back."

"Yes, but to my own place."

"Dear," Flora said, "we so enjoy having you here, but I see that young eagle in you. I understand. I'm finished with your portrait. Would you like to see it?"

"I'd love that."

Flora stood and held out her hand. "Come."

Gabe watched her leave with his mother and his throat tightened. What if she decided not to come back? He was crazy in love with her. He thought he probably had been from the first time she looked up at him from her hospital bed and said, "Blow, Gabriel, blow."

Skye covered his hand with hers. "Don't fret, big brother. She'll come back."

"You have a pipeline of some sort?"

She chuckled. "No, but I have eyes. I think you two are destined for one another, but she needs some time. She needs to find her wings. Be patient."

"Skye's right," Suki said. "I like this one. She's made of sterner stuff than that Lisa critter. Things will work out. You'll see."

Ralph only nodded.

God, Gabe hoped they were right. Losing her would carve a hunk out of his heart. Losing Lisa had been bad, but now he realized that losing Belle would be devastating.

Lisa had been self-centered and obsessed with getting Flora and Skye out of the house and banishing Suki and Ralph to "their place." She'd wanted to be queen of the manor. She'd thought Flora embarrassing and Skye a big baby.

Belle was different. More down-to-earth. And she got along well with his mother and sister. In fact, she seemed to genuinely care for them. Her getting Skye to attend the yoga classes was a miracle in itself. He couldn't imagine Belle ever making him choose between his family obligations and her. It was unthinkable.

But he had to admit, carrying on a courtship under the eyes of his household was a little awkward. Maybe her having a place of her own for a while wouldn't be all bad.

A timber-rattling scream came from upstairs, and Tiger started barking. Gabe shot to his feet and ran for the stairs, Skye, Gus and Ralph on his heels.

"I'll get the broom!" Suki shouted.

Gabe took the steps two at a time and bounded for his mother's studio.

Pale and with her hand at her throat, Flora stood in the middle of the room, Tiger dancing about her feet, still yapping.

"What's wrong?" Gabe asked, looking around for Belle and expecting to see her on the floor surrounded by blood.

"Scorpion," Belle said, walking through the bathroom door. "I stomped it and flushed it down the toilet."

"Thank God." At this rate Gabe figured that his heart might not last until he was forty.

"Guess I don't need the broom," Suki said.

"I just know that I'm a magnet for those nasty bugs," Flora said. "I won't sleep a wink tonight for worrying about one being in my bed."

"They're not bugs," Skye said. "They're arachnids."

Flora fluttered her hand. "Whatever they are, I hate the blasted things. I'm glad that I'm a Pisces and not a Scorpio. I like fish."

Gabe just shook his head.

"I'll spray your rooms good right now," Ralph said.

"And I'll check your bed before you get in it," Belle said.

"Thank you, dear," Flora said, patting Belle's arm. "You're so brave. I'm sorry to be such a scaredy-cat."

"Don't worry about it."

Flora scooped up Tiger, who was still yapping. "Hush now. The emergency is over."

"Is that Belle's portrait?" Gabe asked.

"Yes. It's still drying, so don't touch. I'm rather pleased with it."

"It's spectacular," Belle said hugging Flora. "Thank you."

Everyone else crowded into the studio to look at the painting.

"Would you look at that?" Suki said. "Ain't that something?"

It was indeed something, Gabe thought, his throat tightening. Looking at it touched emotions inside him that he couldn't even name. "I may have to arm wrestle Belle for it. It's beautiful."

"You'll do no such thing, Gabriel," Flora said. "This is Belle's. She can hang it over her fireplace."

"I don't have a fireplace," Belle said, "but I'll find a spot for it."

"I love it," Skye said. "It's one of the most abstract you've ever done, but I can see the beauty and form of her face in this swirl of colors, yet I can also see the power of the young eagle ready to soar to the mountains."

"Exactly," Gabe said. "But what are these things here?" He pointed to several symbols along the sides.

"Those are for Belle to discover," Flora said.

"I'm terrible with symbolism," Belle said. "Just ask my creative writing teacher. He's given up on my efforts at fiction and assigned me a nonfiction project instead."

"What sort of project?" Skye asked.

"I'm writing a brief history of the Outlaw family and their tradition of sticking the kids with notorious outlaw names."

"How fun," Skye said. "I want to read it."

"As do I," Flora said.

"I could probably do a better job if I had my laptop with me. It's stored with my other things at Sam's lake house."

"Is he still in Virginia?" Gabe asked.

"Yes, but he'll be home this weekend. I can get my things next week."

"You should have said you needed a computer," Gabe said. "I've got an extra laptop at the office that I never use. Want to go pick it up now?" He held out his hand to her.

"Sure. Thanks."

Everybody trooped downstairs to watch TV while he and Belle drove to the office.

"I'VE NEVER SEEN your office before," Belle said as they pulled into a parking space in front of the white stone building overlooking the creek. Two security lights on tall poles lit the area, and dim lights were on inside as well.

"I suppose you haven't. Come on in, and I'll give you the grand tour."

"Which side?" She notice that a sign on one half of the building said Burrell Insurance Agency and a sign on the other part said Burrell Real Estate Agency.

"Either one will do. My office is in the back and opens to both." He unlocked the door on the right, and she followed him in. "This is the insurance side. Reception area and offices for three agents."

Lisa must have been at work there as well. Expensive-looking country French chairs in burgundy leather surrounded a coffee table topped with a pot of greenery and neatly placed magazines. A bluebonnet painting hung on one wall and a railroad clock, which looked like an antique, hung on the other. The receptionist's desk was a similar style, as were the others she noticed as they went down the hall.

"The other side is much like this one," he said. "Except that there are four agent offices and a conference room that doubles as a lunchroom."

He led her to his office, unlocked it and turned on the lights. It was just this side of opulent. Large and with built-in bookcases and a credenza, the room sported a huge desk and a black leather chair as well as an arrangement of a couch and chairs in that country French style that screamed *Lisa*. Belle was beginning to hate the stuff.

"Very nice," she said, walking to a window that overlooked the creek, mostly obscured in the dark now, but she could faintly hear the rush of water. The town house that she'd rented was only a block or two away.

Gabe sat at his desk and turned to the doors in the large built-in. He looked in a couple of places before he said, "Ah, here it is." He pulled out a leather case. "Everything you need should be inside."

"Great. Thanks. I'll transcribe my notes tonight. Maybe I'll even get some writing done while I'm gone. I need to interview my dad for sure. Will my driving your car to East Texas be a problem? If it is, I can get a ride to San Marcos and rent one there."

He walked over and stood behind her as she looked out into the darkness of the creek. "I'd like for you to take it. That way I know you'll be back." He locked his arms around her waist and pulled her back against him.

"Oh, I'll be back. Count on it. I love this place."

"Anything else you love here? Anybody else?" He nudged aside her hair and kissed her nape.

"I don't know. Maybe. I'm willing to take some time and see what happens."

"Are we talking about the same thing? I'm talking about us, about you and me."

"So am I. Let's take our time, get to know each other better." She hesitated, then said, "My divorce is final."

He squeezed her waist and nibbled her shoulder. "That's the second-best news I've heard today."

"What's the first-best?"

"That there may be room in your heart for me."

Chapter Fifteen

As she and Skye drove from the house, Belle noticed the llama in the pasture with the lambs. "Carlotta seems more content since you bought the lambs, doesn't she?"

"She was lonely, and the solution has worked out very well, but I didn't buy the lambs."

"You didn't?"

"No. I bartered them for an overdue bill."

"Whatever works. Do you barter things often?"

"Not often, but occasionally. You'd be surprised at some of the things I've accepted in lieu of cash."

"Bet I wouldn't," Belle said. "Kelly, my sister-in-law who's the doctor, delivered a baby last year for a pig."

Skye laughed. "A *pig?* Who got the best deal?"

"My brother would have said the new parents. He had to carry the pig home in his lap."

"How funny."

"It's even funnier to hear Cole tell it."

"I envy your big family. You must miss them."

"I do," Belle said. "Most of the time. But sometimes I

prefer the peace and quiet and privacy of having some distance. Big brothers are quite noisy and extremely bossy."

"I can relate to that."

"Gabe takes his being the head of the household very seriously, doesn't he?"

"Yes, he does, but under the circumstances it's understandable. He blames himself for what happened to me. I was kidnapped when I was in graduate school."

"Oh, no, Skye. I'm sorry. It must have been traumatic."

"Unbelievably so. I don't talk about it much or even remember the worst parts, but it's a miracle that I'm still alive. If Kaiser hadn't attracted attention with his digging and barking, well…. Kaiser was Gus's sire. I loved that dog dearly. He died about two years ago."

Belle itched to hear the rest, but obviously Skye had said all she intended to, and Belle didn't want to push. First time she got hooked up to the Internet, she planned to check it out. "Where did you go to graduate school? A and M?"

"Is there anywhere else? It has one of the best veterinary schools in the country."

"Funny, you don't look like an Aggie," Belle said, teasing.

"I'm a hybrid of major rivals. Undergraduate, I was a tea sipper from the University of Texas. When they face off in football every year, I signal hook 'em, horns, with one hand and gig 'em, Aggies, with the other."

Belle chuckled. "And now you can add— What's the mascot in Wimberley?"

"The Texans."

"Go Texans!" Belle drove her fist toward the windshield.

"Go Texans!" Skye laughed again. "I love having you around. You're so good for me."

"I've loved being around and making a new friend. When I get back, I'm going to take you to the shooting range with Alma, Thelma and me and teach you to shoot."

"I'm not sure if I'm ready for that, but I'm loving yoga."

"Then maybe karate. Are there any martial arts schools in town?" Belle asked as they pulled in front of the center.

"I don't know."

"I'll ask our yoga instructor. I'll bet she knows."

She did, and there was. Belle was glad to hear it. She needed a place to practice and someone to practice with.

AFTER YOGA CLASS and a latte at the coffee shop with Sally, Belle and Skye went home to change. Belle's bags were already packed and the clothes she planned to wear home were laid out. She'd put the laptop Gabe had loaned her in the trunk when they'd left for class this morning, so all she had to do was hang her purse over her shoulder and grab a bag in each hand.

Gabe met her at the foot of the stairs and took the luggage from her. "Why didn't you call me? You shouldn't be lugging these heavy things downstairs."

"Why not? I've got muscles." She did a pose to show off her biceps.

"Yes," he said, dropping a quick kiss on her lips, "but mine are bigger. Ready for some lunch? Skye should be down any minute."

"I thought I'd skip lunch and get on the road. I can grab something at a fast-food place and eat it on the way."

Gabe shook his head.

"No?"

"No," he said. "You need something more nutritious."

After a few stubborn exchanges, she finally compromised and agreed to have lunch with Skye and him, but go in separate cars so that she could leave more quickly after they ate.

"When are you coming back?" Gabe asked.

"Either Sunday evening or sometime Monday. I don't think my missing a ceramics class will put a major kink in my learning curve."

He grinned. "It can't be that bad."

"Trust me. It is. Only my stubbornness is keeping me from dropping the whole thing."

"Naturally, I'd prefer you come back sooner rather than later, but I don't like the idea of your driving alone at night. Wait and come back Monday."

Belle looked at him as if he had three heads and tentacles. "I assure you, Gabe Burrell, that I'm an excellent night driver, and I can handle anything that might happen. I know how to change a tire, and I have a cell phone, a gun and a wrench. I'm not some—" She stopped just short of saying "helpless female" when she noticed Skye coming down the stairs.

"You're not impugning Belle's courage, are you, brother, dear?"

"Not likely I'd survive that," Gabe said. "Ready?"

"Yes, but I can wait until the fight is over."

"We're not fighting, are we, Belle?"

"Blood hasn't been drawn yet, but I'd say we're warming up to it."

"I'll concede," Gabe said. "Let's go eat."

Gabe's SUV led the way, and she followed, waving at Roscoe as she passed by the guard house.

Lunch was pleasant, and they kept Gabe entertained as they described Minnie Strahan's difficulties in the yoga class. Minnie was getting up in years, was at least fifty pounds overweight and had a colorful vocabulary.

Gabe took out a business card, jotted something on the back and handed it to Belle. "These are all the numbers where you can reach me. I put my cell number on the back." He took out another card and poised his pen over it. "Where can I reach you?"

"I'll be staying with my folks at the Double Dip."

"And the number is…?"

Rather than shoot him a smart reply, she gave him the number of the shop as well as her cell number.

They all walked out together to their cars. Skye kissed her cheek and said, "Be safe. See you in a few days."

Skye got in the SUV, and Gabe lingered while Belle unlocked the car. "I'll miss you," he said.

"I'll miss you, too. All of you. Your family has been wonderful to me."

He gave her a brief kiss. "Call me."

"I will."

When she drove out of Wimberley toward San Marcos, Belle felt a little weepy to be leaving. Silly. She'd be back in three or four days. In the short time since she'd arrived, it had become home.

As SHE WAS PASSING through San Marcos, Belle saw a huge sign on a portable marquee.

Designer Furniture Outlet. Sale! Sale! Everything must go! 75-90% off!

The ad reminded her that she had a town house—but no furniture. Not even a bed or a chair. She'd sold almost everything when she'd moved in with Matt. She had office furniture, a TV and kitchen stuff in storage at Sam's lake house, but no mattress.

That marquee was fate talking to her.

First chance she had, Belle made a U-turn and headed back to the furniture store.

She found the answer to her prayers. This was the first day of the sale, so she had a good selection and a saleswoman named Jo Marie who seemed to know furniture.

"What style do you like?" Jo Marie asked. "We have some lovely country French pieces."

"*No* country French. I like anything but country French. I want something bright and cheerful and comfortable. And I insist on a great mattress. By the way, can you deliver it to Wimberley tomorrow or Saturday?"

"Tomorrow. No problem."

Belle had an extra key that they could use to deliver and place the furniture, then they could leave the key with Sally at the beauty salon.

In no time she'd bought a bed and mattress, a nightstand, a dresser, a chair and a couple of lamps for her bedroom, a simple dining set with a round table and four chairs, a scrumptious red sectional couch with a chaise, an easy chair, occasional tables and an entertainment armoire for her TV and stereo equipment when she retrieved it from Sam. A couple more lamps for the living room and eventual office area in the second bedroom and a few gorgeous decorative pillows that were dirt cheap, and she had all the basics.

There was a really great rug for a steal that Jo Marie talked her into. She said it tied the colors of her living room furniture together and gave it a finished look. God forbid that she wouldn't have a finished look in her living room. She could add accessories later.

In less than forty-five minutes, she'd bought furniture for her whole place, made arrangements for its delivery the next day, drew a map for furniture placement, written the check and was on the road again.

Gabe's ex-fiancée couldn't have done that. It probably took her days to select just the right pillow or lamp.

Eat your heart out, Lisa baby.

Chapter Sixteen

It was almost eight o'clock when Belle arrived in Naconiche. She'd called her parents and told them when she'd crossed the county line.

"Have you had dinner?" her mother asked.

"No, I haven't."

"Good, because I have a meat loaf ready."

"With tomato sauce?" Belle asked.

"Of course. And mashed potatoes and fresh green beans."

"With toasted almonds?"

"Naturally. Your father will leave the door unlocked downstairs."

The meal her mother described had been her favorite as far back as she could remember. Nobody made meat loaf like Nonie Outlaw. And she would bet her last dollar that there would be a fudge pie waiting on the table.

It was good to be going home to her family.

She was ready.

And she didn't have to worry about wrestling her bags inside. Her dad was waiting by the curb in front of the Double Dip when she pulled up. Thicker at the waist and grayer than when he was sheriff of Naconiche County, Wes Outlaw was still the big handsome man with the warm smile that she adored. She threw her arms around him and reveled in the scent of Old Spice and starched shirt. He hugged her back with a familiarity that brought tears in a quick sting. That hug from his bearlike arms always assured her that everything would be all right. Everything.

"It's good to have you home, baby girl."

"It's good to be home, Dad. I've missed you."

"Well, come on in. Your mother's waiting on pins and needles. Baked you a meat loaf and a fudge pie. Need any help with your bags?"

"I could use a strong back, old man."

"Who're you calling an old man, missy? I can still turn you over my knee."

Belle laughed. "You've never turned me over your knee in your life. My bags are in the trunk." She popped it open with the remote.

"Lot of stuff for the weekend. You staying longer, I hope?"

"No, not this time. Sorry. Actually, we can leave this one in the trunk. I'll just need the smaller one, and I'll get the laptop."

"I'll get it. Fancy wheels you're driving," her dad said. "Rental?"

"No. It belongs to a friend."

"Must be a good friend. Friend you've been staying with?"

She kissed his cheek. "Once a cop, always a cop. I'll explain everything later. I'm starving. I've been smelling that meat loaf since I crossed the river bridge."

The bell on the front door jingled as they went inside the

ice-cream parlor, and Nonie Outlaw came flying down the steps from their apartment, arms open wide.

"Hi, Mama," Belle said, taking the shorter, white-haired woman into her arms. Five pounds of tension dropped away.

After they hugged, Nonie took Belle's face in her hands and scanned her features. "You still look a little gaunt. Have you lost weight? Are you well?"

"I'm finer than frog fur, Mama. I promise. A doctor who used to be Kelly's teacher pronounced me fit."

"She looks good to me, Nonie," her dad said. "I locked the front door, and I'm gonna take these bags upstairs. Let's eat. Belle's hungry, and my belly's about stuck to my backbone."

Her mother laughed and led Belle upstairs. "No such thing, Wes Outlaw. You belly has a long way to go before it clears your belt buckle."

Her parents didn't quiz her anymore before dinner. They caught her up on family and town doings while they ate. It wasn't until Belle demolished the last bite of fudge pie that Wes asked casually, "How's Matt?"

Belle put her fork down and took a deep breath. "I don't know. Matt and I are divorced."

"Divorced?" Her mother looked at Wes. "Didn't I tell you something was wrong there?"

"You did. Want to tell us about it?"

Belle sketched the facts for them.

"Sorry son of a bitch!"

"Wes! Watch your language."

"I did. I was thinking worse."

Belle laughed. "I said and thought worse myself. I must have had the shortest marriage on record."

"No, I think some movie star's got you beat," her mother said. "Good riddance, I say. I always thought he had a shifty look."

"Thought that myself," her dad said. "You going to try to get your old job back?"

She shook her head. "No. I'm not sure I could if I wanted to, and I don't. The FBI's not for me."

"Naconiche still needs a chief of police," Wes said. "Council can't agree on anybody. Bet you'd be a shoo-in. I can talk to the mayor tomorrow."

"Thanks, but no thanks. I'm not sure yet what I'm going to do. I plan to take my time, but I think I may settle in Wimberley. I like it there, and I've rented a town house."

Her mother's eyebrows went up, a sure sign of her built-in radar. "There wouldn't already be a man in the picture, would there?"

"Maybe. Maybe not. I'm certainly not going to jump back into another bad marriage any time soon."

"Glad to hear that," Wes said. "You bring the next one around for the family to inspect before you get too tangled up."

"I'll do that, Sheriff." Belle stood and kissed his forehead on her way to fetch the coffeepot.

Later, after she'd pled exhaustion, which wasn't an exaggeration, Belle got ready for bed in the guest room. She'd just climbed between the covers with her book when there was a light tapping on the door.

"Come in."

Her mother stuck her head in. "Am I interrupting?"

"Never." Belle patted the bed beside her.

"Sweetheart, I'm so sorry about what happened with Matt.

I know you loved him or you would never have married him. And I know that his betrayal hurt you deeply. Loyalty was always a critical issue with you. And while you always act tough, I know you have a tender heart."

Despite her best effort a tear welled up and trickled from her left eye. Her mother gathered Belle into her arms as if she were a child and rocked her gently.

More tears came, and another five pounds of tension melted away.

THE NEXT MORNING Belle was helping in the shop when her brother J.J. came in.

"Morning," Belle said, "did you come in for a cup of coffee?"

"Coffee would be nice, but I came in to see you and hug your neck. I haven't seen you since Christmas, and that wasn't for long. Come here." He wrapped her in a huge hug. All the Outlaw men were extra tall and were big huggers, some more that others. He took a seat at the counter.

Before she could get J.J.'s coffee poured, Frank came in from the courthouse across the street. Both he and J.J. had their offices there. Frank, too, demanded a hug.

"Coffee?" she asked.

"I don't have time. I just declared a ten-minute recess to come see you. We can talk more at lunch." He glanced to J.J.

"I just got here," J.J. said. "I haven't had time to invite her."

"Invite me where?"

"Mary Beth wanted the family to come to the tea room for a late lunch. She said to come around one when the last of the noon crowd is clearing out. She's fixing something special," J.J. said.

Mary Beth was very proud of her business, the successful Twilight Tea Room and the adjacent Twilight Inn Motel.

"Sounds wonderful," Belle said. "Is she up to it?" Both Mary Beth and Carrie were over six months pregnant.

"Sure. She takes it easy and has a great staff."

"You can ride with Carrie and me," Frank said. "Her office is just over there." He pointed to a spot catty-cornered across the square from the Double Dip. "Listen, I gotta get back to court. I'll see you about five till. Carrie said she'd meet me here." He kissed her cheek and hurried out the door.

"What about Cole and Kelly?" Belle asked J.J.

"Kelly has arranged her schedule so that, barring an emergency, she can drop by for a while, and Cole has the afternoon off, so he'll be there with Elizabeth. Dad's picking up Katy and the twins from school and keeping them to give us some time to talk."

"But I want to see my nieces and nephew," Belle said.

"Don't worry. You'll see plenty of them over the weekend. Carrie and Frank are having everybody over on Saturday for a cookout, and Kelly and Cole are throwing something on Sunday."

"I feel like visiting royalty."

"You are, princess." He took a sip of coffee, then set down his cup. "Belle, Mom told us about the divorce. Rather, she told me, and I told Mary Beth and Frank and Carrie. Cole's in class, and Kelly is with patients or I would have told them. I sure am sorry about it."

"Thanks, J.J. It's simply one of those awful things that happen."

"Another locked bathroom in the pathway of life."

She laughed. "I'm not sure the analogy fits, but yeah. That just about covers it. I got sick on my way home from Colorado, and Sam and a friend of his flew up and got me."

"Why didn't you call me? I could have picked you up and brought you home."

"I didn't want to take you or Frank or Cole away from your families. As it was, I had to spend several days in the hospital, then Sam's friend flew me to Wimberley in his helicopter, and I've been staying with his family while Sam was in Virginia."

"Are you doing okay? You ought to have Kelly check you out."

"I'm fine now, J.J. Really."

"Good. Well, I guess I'd better get back to my office in case any bad guys are on the prowl. Thanks for the coffee."

"The coffee isn't mine. It belongs to the Double Dip. Here's your bill." She scratched a number on a guest check and slapped it on the counter.

"But Mom doesn't charge me—"

"I'm not Mom. Pay up, big boy."

He grinned and tossed a couple of bills on the counter. "Keep the change."

"Don't think I won't," she shouted after him.

He only laughed and waved before he trotted across the street.

COLE STOOD BY THE DOOR of the tea room waiting for Belle and grabbed her the moment she walked in. She hugged him fiercely.

"Good to see you, Ding-dong."

"And it's good to see you, big buzzer." Cole was special,

larger-than-life in her eyes, and the one who'd always been her protector.

"I think the Outlaw brothers ought to load up the pickup, go to Colorado and whip that sorry bastard's ass."

Belle laughed. "Sam already offered. I think we ought to forget that he ever lived."

"You're on."

"Stop hogging my sister-in-law, Cole," Kelly said. "And take Elizabeth while I get my hug." She thrust their baby at him and embraced Belle. "It's good to have you home. J.J. said you've been ill."

"A nasty case of pneumonia, but I've been pronounced well by Dr. Kaye Hamilton. She said to tell you hello."

"Kaye Hamilton? That's great. You've been in good hands."

Mary Beth, still in her yellow apron, was there next. They hugged and Mary Beth drew her to a seat at the head of a long table that had been put together. Only a couple of stragglers occupied other tables.

Mary Beth's staff served lunch, and the Outlaw clan, sans Sam, talked nonstop. Kelly had to get back to patients, so Belle held Elizabeth with one arm and ate dessert with the other. She had a grand time.

It was good to be home.

But as much as she loved her family, she thought later as she walked alone around the square, she wouldn't want to move back here permanently. She wanted to make her own way somewhere else.

Wally's feed store still stood on the corner and acted as the bus stop. There was the drugstore, the antique store, the City Grill. She crossed the street and went in the law offices of

Murdock and Outlaw. Since Carrie had joined the practice, Mr. Murdock had cut his hours back. Things were quiet when Belle went inside, so the receptionist sent her right in.

"I came to pick up my papers."

Carrie opened a drawer and pulled out the envelope. "Here they are, and I didn't tell a soul."

"Thanks. I appreciate it, but everybody knows now. Are you really on to go shopping with Mary Beth and me tomorrow morning?"

"Oh, yeah. I don't think I've ever been to a garage sale. It should be fun. Mary Beth is a garage sale fiend. Trust her to find whatever you need for the new place. I'm only sorry that Kelly has to work. She's been open on Saturday mornings for a while to make up for some of the other mornings she takes off to be with the baby."

"Are you sure you're going to have time to shop and host the cookout that afternoon?"

Carrie winked at her. "That's the advantage of having a cookout and a housekeeper. She's making the side dishes, and Frank's grilling the meat." She patted her tummy. "Plus being pregnant exempts me from a lot. All I have to do is fold the napkins and be gracious. My kind of party. Mary Beth says we should start early to get the best stuff. We'll pick you up at seven-thirty."

"You're on. Is there any news on the oil drilling?"

"My uncle says it's looking fantastic. We have every hope of bringing in a good well in a few weeks."

"I hope so. I may need the income until I decide what I want to do careerwise."

"We can use another lawyer here."

Belle shook her head. "Thanks, but I'm going into something totally away from anything to do with the law."

"Going to rebel against the Outlaw tradition?"

"Looks like I am. I read once in a psychology class that the youngest child is usually the maverick. I guess that's me."

"Good for you. Any prospects?"

"I'm exploring all sorts of things. I may even see a career counselor when I get back to Wimberley." Belle stood. "Thanks for keeping these papers for me. I'll see you in the morning."

"WOULD YOU TAKE twenty dollars for all of this?" Mary Beth asked.

The woman thought for a minute. "I'll sell it for twenty-five and throw in the bath mat."

"It's a deal," Belle said, pulling the cash from her bag. She was now the proud owner of a lovely designer bedspread and pillow shams, as well as a shower curtain and bath mat.

She, Carrie and Mary Beth hoisted her loot and took it out to the car.

"I could have gotten this for twenty," Mary Beth said.

"I would have paid the fifty she was asking," Belle said. "It's a bargain. I'm so glad she decided to redecorate her guest room."

"What else is on your list?" Carrie asked.

"I need some towels and enough kitchen things to make do until I can get my things from Sam's place. A can opener, a couple of spoons and a pot will do it. I can use paper plates and plastic utensils for a while."

"I've got a bunch of stuff like that out in the barn," Carrie told her. "Things I stored there when I sold my place in

Houston. I sold all the furniture with it, or I could offer you that. Knives. I've got some knives you can have."

"Let's see what we can find at the next couple of sales, but we might have to drive over to Travis Lake to the outlet linen store for the towels," Mary Beth said. "That's were I got all of ours. And you'll want something pretty and matching, not some raggedy old things."

They didn't find any towels, but they did pick up several kitchen items for just a few dollars and lots of doodads like candlesticks and decorative baskets. The car trunk was full before they drove to Travis Lake.

Mary Beth zeroed in on some high-end towels that matched the shower curtain and bath mat and were perfect for her new place. Best of all, they were a fraction of their original cost. Belle also bought bed pillows and sheets and a couch throw.

"This ought to do it," Belle said.

"With the stuff from me, you should have everything," Carrie said. "Come a little early this afternoon, and we'll check out the boxes in the barn."

They had finished all their shopping and were home before one. Belle adored her sisters-in-law. She and Carrie had now been introduced to the amazing world of garage sales. How had she missed them for so long?

She thought of Lisa buying decorative accessories from tables in somebody's garage and snorted. Lisa didn't know what she was missing. Wonder where she was now? How likely was she to show up on Gabe's doorstep wanting to rekindle their old relationship?

The thought of it happening to her again sent cold chills over her. She couldn't take it a second time. Now that she had some distance from Gabe, maybe it was time to rethink the whole situation.

If she were honest and objective, she couldn't see herself living permanently with Gabe in a house decorated by his ex-fiancée and shared with two other women. Three, if you counted Suki. While she adored Flora and Skye, she wouldn't want to live with them on a permanent basis. She wouldn't want to live with her own mother, much less Gabe's.

His house wouldn't be her house, and thinking of sleeping in a bed where he'd made love to another woman struck Belle as creepy.

No way. She'd simply forget about there ever being the possibility of marriage and concentrate on having a long-term affair. Maybe like Violet Anders, who owned the florist shop in Naconiche. She'd "kept company" with Chuck Blankenship for over thirty years, and they'd seemed happy as clams. Sounded like a perfect solution to her.

And in any case, any idea of marriage talk was months away. She had to get herself headed in the right direction before she could consider any other commitment.

ABOUT MID-AFTERNOON, Belle drove to Carrie and Frank's house, the house where she grew up. Her parents were coming over in a hour or so when her mother's helper showed up to take over the Double Dip. On her way there she phoned Sally to see if the furniture had been delivered. It had.

"The guy brought the key to me yesterday afternoon about three," Sally said. "I'm dying to see what all you bought."

"I'll invite you over when I get everything in place."

"Good deal. I've got to run and check a color."

"Okay. 'Bye. And thanks."

Belle pulled to a stop outside the big, rambling Victorian that her grandfather had built. She thought about calling Gabe, but the front door flew open and the twins, Janey and Jimmy, came flying out the door yelling, "Aunt Belle's here!"

She got out of the car and hugged both of them. "How could you grow so much in such a short time? Will you be starting high school next year?"

They giggled.

"No. We'll be in first grade," Janey said.

Belle feigned shock. "I don't believe it."

"Believe what?" Carrie asked.

"Aunt Belle thought we'd be in high school next year 'cause we've growed so much," Jimmy said, flashing a gap-toothed smile.

Carrie laughed. "You two go help Daddy. Aunt Belle and I are going to check something in the barn."

The twins ran off, and she and Carrie headed for the barn, where everything under the sun was stored. They sorted through three big boxes of stuff and came up with several things that Belle could use, including a set of very nice knives, a cookie sheet, two pots and a frying pan. She also produced place mats and napkins and kitchen towels.

"How about this alarm clock?" Carrie said. "And this set of bookends? Do you have an iron?"

"I'll take the alarm clock and the iron. I have bookends at Sam's. Let's put this in the car and go help Frank."

"Good idea. The twins are probably driving him crazy with their help."

"Carrie, may I ask you a personal question?"

"Sure. Shoot."

"How did you cope with sleeping in a bed that Frank's first wife had slept in?"

"Poorly. Especially when I had to look at a wedding picture of her staring down at me."

"You're kidding," Belle said as they lugged stuff to her car.

"Only a little. That was before we got married. Long before. We changed bedrooms and bought new bedroom furniture. And I had a lot of stuff in the house recovered. We bought some new things together. Are you seeing a widower?"

Belle shook her head. "I just wondered."

Before they could say more, J.J. and Mary Beth arrived with Mary Beth's daughter Katy, who was the same age as the twins.

Right behind them were Cole and Kelly, carrying Elizabeth in her car seat. Belle waved to everybody just as her cell phone rang.

"Hi, there, gorgeous," Gabe said. "I sure do miss you."

Belle walked away from the crowd and stood by a huge pine tree in the front yard. "I miss you, too. How's everybody?"

"We're all fine. Everybody misses you. Carlotta sends her regards."

Belle laughed. "I'll bet."

"How is your visit going?"

"Great. As a matter of fact I'm at a family gathering at my brother Frank's house and the clan Outlaw is arriving."

"Then I'd better let you go. Any idea when you'll be home yet?"

"Not exactly. There are plans tomorrow, so it depends on what time the festivities are over and how tired I am."

"Take care."

"I will."

Her mom and dad arrived as she hung up, and everybody went inside, then out onto the large patio where Frank was firing up the grill. J.J. and Cole handed out drinks while the kids romped and Belle kept everybody laughing with her tale about Carlotta, the llama who rang doorbells.

They all wanted to know more about the family she'd stayed with, so she told them a bit about Gabe and Flora and Skye and the broom-wielding Suki and her husband Ralph.

Cole handed her a glass of wine and whispered, "Was it Gabe that you were talking to on your cell phone earlier?"

She looked startled. "Yes. How did you know?"

"Because you had the same dreamy-eyed expression then that you have talking about him now."

"I *don't* have a dreamy-eyed expression. That's ridiculous."

"I know you too well, Ding-dong. Just don't jump into anything too quickly."

"Why is it that people are always saying that to me? Don't you think I have a lick of sense?"

Cole threw up his hands. "Erase that. Want a peanut?"

SEEING ALL THE FAMILY was wonderful, but she was soon tuckered out. After dinner she went home and slept like the dead.

Brunch the next day was more intimate. While her parents went to church, she joined Cole and Kelly at their house. Cole was making omelets, and Kelly had just taken a coffee cake from the oven when the phone rang.

"What you want to bet that Brittany Jackson is having

her baby? Right now?" Kelly said, then answered the phone. She asked a few questions, then hung up. "I was right. I'm so sorry, Belle, but I have to go. I don't know when I'll be back."

Belle kissed Kelly's cheek. "No problem. Big buzzer and I will do justice to this lovely meal. Can't you eat a bite?"

Kelly shook her head. "I'll eat a breakfast bar on the way." She gave Cole a quick kiss. "I'll call later."

She and Cole enjoyed their time together. Elizabeth was napping, so they ate and talked about what she might do in terms of a job.

"I'd suggest talking to a career counselor. There are some great ones at the junior college where I teach. They might give you some insights."

"I'd thought about that already. I may check out somebody when I get back to Wimberley, which," she said as she looked at her watch, "might be before dark if I get a move on. Let's get the dishes done."

"I'll do the dishes," Cole said. "I'd rather you not be on the road after dark."

She laughed. "You sound like Gabe."

Cole grinned. "Smart man. I'm anxious to meet him."

"You'll like him. Sam does."

"That's no recommendation. Sam likes everybody."

After she left Cole, Belle went back to the Double Dip and packed her car. By the time her parents arrived home, she was ready to go.

"I was hoping that you could stay longer," her mother said.

"I will next time, but I'm eager to get back and see how all my new stuff looks in the town house."

"You know I'd like for you to hang around a whole lot longer, baby girl," her dad said, "but if you're set on leaving today, I'd rather you weren't on the—"

"Road after dark," Belle said along with him.

How many protective men did a girl need?

Chapter Seventeen

As she approached San Marcos, it dawned on Belle that her cupboard was totally bare. She wheeled into the parking lot of the first large grocery store she saw and filled her cart with a few essentials, including paper products for kitchen and bath, disposable dishes and plastic utensils. Since she didn't have her coffeepot yet—and had forgotten to get one in her rounds—instant coffee was a necessary evil. But the thought of it made her gag, so she went looking for a coffeepot. Luckily she found a four-cup automatic and tossed it in the basket with a couple of frozen dinners, eggs, butter, milk, bread, salt and pepper, sliced turkey and cheese from the deli, and a real deal can of coffee. She added a bagged salad and some fruit from the produce section and called it done. She'd make a list the next day and stock the pantry and fridge properly.

She was loading her bags in the car, tucking them here and there among all the other items she'd hauled home, when her cell phone rang.

She glanced at the caller ID. Gabe.

"Hi, there," she said. "What's up?"

"I was wondering about your ETA," he said. "I talked with

your mom a few minutes ago, and she said that you had a car full of stuff. I thought you might need some help unloading."

"I won't say no to help. I'm beat after the long drive. I should be at my town house in about fifteen or twenty minutes, and I need to get the bed made so that I'll have a place to sleep."

"You always have a place to sleep, you know. I was hoping you might stay with us a while longer, until you have things ready."

"Things will be ready enough by bedtime. Do you know the address?"

He hesitated. "Yes. I even know the color of your new couch. I think most of the town knows by now. Mother's been looking through her stacks of paintings to find the ones with a splash of red."

Eighteen minutes later, Belle pulled to a stop outside her new place. Gabe leaned against his fender, waiting.

He opened her car door and bent down for a kiss. "Welcome home."

He grabbed a box and a couple of bags while she unlocked the front door and turned on the lights.

"Say," he said, "this is nice. Where do you want this stuff?"

"All that goes in the kitchen."

Belle started back out the door, but Gabe said, "Why don't you put up, and I'll tote."

"Good plan. Bring the grocery bags first." She made a quick trip through the rooms and was pleased with the furniture arrangement.

In the kitchen, she found the fridge on and humming, so she stashed the perishables first and stowed the rest of the groceries in the pantry and cabinet.

"Where does this stuff go?" Gabe asked, his arms full of outlet bags and garage sale items.

"In the bedroom for now," she said, carrying a bundle of toilet tissue to the bathroom.

In the bedroom she found the sheets for the bed and opened the package. She'd like to be able to wash the sheets and towels, but she forgot to get soap for the washing machine. They would do. She also realized as she fanned out the bottom sheet that she'd failed to get a mattress protector, too. Oh, well.

"Let me help you with that," Gabe said.

"You know how to make a bed?"

"Of course I know how. We didn't always have a house-keeper, and Flora was never very good with such chores."

He was better at bed-making than she was. His corners were all military straight. He sacked up the pillows in their cases while she unfolded the soft gold damask bedspread. The woman who'd sold it to her said it was freshly laundered, so she felt good about using it.

"This is really pretty," Gabe said as he helped her spread it over the bed.

"Thanks. It only cost about twenty dollars. I bought it at a garage sale."

He stopped dead still. "A garage sale? Belle, I would have bought you a bedspread."

She laughed. "But I wouldn't have had as much fun as I had shopping with Carrie and Mary Beth. I love bargains. Why, I spent less than an hour and just over fifteen hundred dollars on all the furniture. And it's good stuff that I bought in a close-out sale in San Marcos. Did you sit on the couch yet? It's very comfortable."

He flopped on the bed. "I don't know about the couch, but the bed's comfortable."

"Get up, you doofus! You're wrinkling it."

He laughed and pulled her down beside him. "I've been itching to get you into bed."

His mouth covered hers, and she simply melted. In a nanosecond, every thought she'd had, every vow she'd made to take things slow with Gabe, evaporated.

His hand slipped under her shirt to cup her breast, and she moaned. His tongue stroked hers, and she went crazy. His fingers popped open the button of her jeans, and she was all over him like a wild woman.

"I don't have any protection with me, do you?"

"No."

Breathing hard, he threw himself on his back. Breathing just as hard, she lay beside him.

"Damn," he said.

"Damn," she echoed, then laughed.

He started laughing, too. Then he stood. "On your feet, woman, we've got to finish getting this bed made." He grabbed an extra pillow and crammed it into the sham.

She rearranged her clothes and took a bag of towels to the bathroom. He put up the shower curtain while she finished with the other kitchen items and living room accessories. The place was beginning to look great.

"You about done for tonight?" he asked. "Want to go out for dinner?"

"I'm too pooped to go out, and I have frozen dinners and salad. Want one?"

"Sure, let me wash up."

"Uh-oh," she said.

"What?"

"I don't have any soap. No hand soap, no bath soap, no dish soap, no washing machine soap. I totally forgot about soap."

"Tell you what. You handle the cooking, and I'll go out on soap patrol. Be right back."

Belle cleared the dining table and laid out a pair of Carrie's place mats along with paper napkins and plastic knives and forks. In the center she put a garage sale candle—but she didn't have any matches and her range was electric. She waited a few minutes, then put the frozen dinners in the microwave and fixed the salads in paper bowls.

Gabe came through the door just as the microwave beeped.

"Perfect timing," she said. "You want spaghetti or chicken florentine?"

"Either is fine." He set the two paper bags he carried on the counter and started unloading them. "I got hand soap for kitchen and bath, some of that all-purpose squirt stuff, two kinds of bath soap, dishwasher soap, powder and liquid, and washing machine soap, powder and liquid."

She laughed. "Why so much?"

"I wasn't sure what kind you liked, so I gave you choices. And I bought a pie. Lemon chess. You like lemon chess?"

"I love lemon chess."

"Good. They were out of chocolate and pecan."

He turned on the faucet, held out the pump bottle and squirted a dollop of melon-scented soap onto her hands and his.

"I can offer you water or milk."

"How about wine?" He fished a bottle from the sack.

"No corkscrew."

"Now that I'm prepared for." He pulled out a Swiss Army knife, found the corkscrew and opened the bottle while she slid the dinners onto paper plates.

Belle took the dinners to the dining table, and Gabe brought the wine and plastic glasses. He even found a book of matches in his car and lit the candle.

"To your new home," Gabe said, touching his glass to hers.

She couldn't remember when she'd enjoyed a meal more.

THANK GOODNESS Belle had set the alarm clock that Carrie had given her because she'd gone to sleep with her book in her hands and her bedside light still on. She reminded herself to put lightbulbs on her list. She'd stolen one from the chandelier over the dining table to put in the bedroom lamp.

After a quick breakfast of coffee and leftover lemon chess pie, she showered and made it to ceramics class in time to further humiliate herself with the potter's wheel. She was getting better, but not much. She went to lunch with Alma, Thelma and Steve and enjoyed the free margarita more than usual.

Her phone rang as she was leaving the Mexican restaurant, but instead of Gabe, it was Flora inviting her over to select some artwork for her house. She promised to stop by in half an hour, after she'd finished making a list of necessities.

The list grew longer and longer. She was about to leave when there was a knock on the door. It was Sally with her key and a big wrapped box with a purple bow.

"I only have a minute before my next appointment," Sally said, "but I wanted to bring you a housewarming gift."

"How sweet of you. Come in and see the place. It's not finished yet, but I'm getting there."

"How darling! I love the red couch. You have all the basics, and half the fun is taking your time and finding just the right accessories. This candelabra is gorgeous."

"Thanks. I got it at a garage sale in Naconiche for three dollars." Belle set the box on the table and tore off the wrapping.

"Don't you just love garage sales?"

"Now I do." She opened the box and took out a beautiful, sleek spice rack, filled with spices of every kind. "Oh, Sally, this is fantastic. I don't have anything but salt and pepper. Thank you."

"You're welcome. The kitchen shop on the square has all sorts of goodies that you might need. Check them out. I've gotta run now. I'll see you Thursday if not before."

Belle grabbed her bag and her list and went out with Sally. Then she had to go back inside and pick up a box of gifts she'd brought back from Naconiche.

The drive through the guard gate was achingly familiar. She waved to Roscoe and drove to the house.

Suki answered the door. "Good to see you, Belle. Need some help with that box?"

"No, I've got it. I have presents for everybody."

"Did I hear presents?" Flora asked as she came downstairs. "I love presents."

"They're not wrapped, but I hope you like them. I found things that were typically Naconiche." She carried the box back to the den to open it. "A man there makes beautiful things from old cedar fence posts. Like this weed pot for you."

Belle handed Flora the wooden, thin-necked vase that was still gnarled and rough on most of the bottom, but about halfway up, the cedar was beautifully turned and burnished to a high gloss. There was room only for three thin stems of dried flowers.

"Oh, it's lovely," Flora said. "Reminds me of a phoenix rising from the ashes."

"Ain't that something!" Suki said.

"I brought one for you, too, Suki. And thank you for all you did taking care of me."

"Gee willerkers, I didn't do anything special. But I thank you anyhow."

"As do I," Flora said, sniffing the weed pot. "I can smell the cedar."

"I brought a votive candle holder for Skye that's in the same style, and I gave Gabe a pencil cup for his desk last night. And I brought homemade preserves and jelly for everybody. Fig and peach preserves as well as dewberry and mayhaw jelly. I particularly want Maria and Manuel to have some fig preserves. A friend of my mother's makes the best in the county. And I heard Ralph say that he liked peach."

"He does," Suki said. "He'll be tickled."

Flora hugged her. "This is so sweet of you, dear. Come up to the studio and help me pick out some paintings for your walls. I have tons of them in the closet and against the wall. I've picked out a few that I think you might like. I'm going to put my weed pot on my dresser."

Belle couldn't believe her luck. Flora insisted on giving her three large oils, in addition to her portrait, that would be perfect for her house. She'd need frames, but she could hang them without for the time being.

As soon as she got a hammer.

And some of those hanger doodads.

SOME GUYS WOULD HAVE brought her roses. Gabe showed up with a potted plant in a fabulous container for her coffee table.

"I love it," Belle said. "What is it?"

Gabe took a slip from his pocket. "It's a spathiphyllum, better known as a closet plant. I understand they're almost indestructible. Feed it occasionally and water it if it begins to look a little droopy and don't put it in direct sunlight. Here are the directions."

She put it on the table. It brought new life to the room. "It looks great there. Plants really make a difference, don't they? I want to get a big one for that corner in the dining room."

"I'll get you one. What kind do you want?"

"Maybe a ficus or a palm. I'm not in to plant names much. I thought that I would go to a nursery and find one I like."

"We can go tomorrow and pick out one."

"Don't you have to work?"

"I'm the boss. I don't have to work if I don't want to. Besides, how long can it take to find a plant? We'll hit the nursery tomorrow morning, and then you can go with me while I take a client up in the chopper in the afternoon. I'm showing a couple from Houston some property. Set out the paper plates. I have a surprise for dinner. It's in the car."

"A surprise? What?"

"If I tell you, it's not a surprise."

She set the table while he retrieved two insulated packs.

"In this one we have beer." He unzipped the case and drew out two cold bottles. "And in this one, we have four dozen tamales and a bowl of frijoles that Maria fixed."

"*Four* dozen?"

"Maria said what we don't eat, you can put in the freezer."

"Gabe Burrell, you are a gem among men."

"Hold that thought."

The tamales were to die for, and there were plenty left for the freezer. After dinner, they both sat down on the new red couch, kicked off their shoes and propped their feet on the new glass coffee table.

"Want to watch some TV?" Gabe asked.

"I don't have a TV."

"I thought that was for a TV." He pointed to the Asian-inspired armoire across from the couch.

"It is, but there's no TV in it."

"I'll buy you a TV."

She laughed and swatted his thigh. "No, you won't. I have a perfectly good one with my stuff at Sam's."

"When are we going to get your stuff?"

"We don't have to. Sam and a couple of his buddies are moving some of his things to San Antonio this weekend, and they're going to drop off my boxes and my SUV on their way."

"Good. Is Sam selling the lake house?"

"No, he's going to keep it and maybe rent it out occasionally."

"Maybe we can go up sometime and go fishing. You like to fish?"

"I *love* to fish. I even learned to fly fish when I was in Colorado. Got pretty good at it, too."

Gabe hugged her against him. "Is there anything you can't do?"

She slipped her arms around his waist. "Sure. I can't sing on key, play the piano or throw a pot worth a damn. I can't ride a skateboard or bake a cake fit to eat or draw anything more than a stick figure. My efforts at fiction are laughable, and my poetry sucks. I'm a dismal failure at sewing of any kind, and I'm terrible at charades."

He laughed and dropped a quick kiss on her nose. "Besides that?"

"I can't yodel."

"That's a shame." He kissed her lips. "Anything else?"

"Lots of things, but I can't seem to remember them right now." Her brain was clouded with yearning as she strained toward him and threaded her fingers through his hair, pulling his mouth closer against hers and savoring the urgency sparking between them.

He tugged at her shirt, and she tugged at his, their hands urgent, their breaths hard and fast.

He pulled back, and she whimpered, her lips trying to follow him.

"Let's go to your bed," Gabe said. "I dreamed about those sheets, and I want our first time to be perfect. We'll christen the couch another time." He pulled her to her feet and led her to the bedroom.

Or maybe she led him. She wasn't sure. She was only sure that she was eager to get there. He pulled her T-shirt over her head and unsnapped her jeans as her fingers fumbled for his shirt buttons. First the sound of her zipper, then his.

His mouth never left hers as he kicked off his pants, dragged back the spread and lay her on the sheets.

He murmured love words and words of praise for her body as he tossed aside her bra and explored her breasts. There wasn't a place on her that he didn't touch with hands or lips or tongue, and she reveled in the sensations overwhelming her body.

She stripped off the rest of his clothes in a frenzy and rolled him onto his back. On fire, she straddled his hips.

"Wait, love," he moaned.

She yanked open the drawer of the bedside table and grabbed a condom. "Here." She fumbled, trying to open it.

"I'll do it."

"Hurry."

He chuckled. "Believe me, I'm hurrying."

As soon as he was done, she plunged herself onto him. The sensation bowed her back and sucked the breath from her. She started to move. Beneath her fingertips, his muscles trembled with tension. Hers trembled as well, her body begged for release. Demanded it. She contracted her muscles and ground herself against him.

"Don't move," he said, grasping her hips to still her. "Give me a second."

"To hell with that." She moved.

He moved.

An orgasm hit her that shook the rafters. His must have been at the same magnitude because he let out a groan, a mating cry that sent another thrill racing to her core.

They were still for a moment, then his hands moved gently over her hips and her breasts. "I knew it would be like this for us. I only wish it had lasted longer."

She smiled and stroked both hands over his chest. "Why? Do you need to leave now?"

He laughed, and she could feel it inside her. "Sweetheart, you couldn't get me out with a pry pole. Got any pie left?"

"You're thinking about pie at a time like this?"

"I need something to keep up my strength."

"That's my boy."

Chapter Eighteen

Belle went around with a sappy smile on her face for the next few days. Her good sense kept trying to tell her to slow down and be cautious in her involvement with Gabe, but she told her good sense to shut up. She adored him. And he made her feel desirable again—not like a loser. Sure, there might be problems if he started mentioning the M word. Lots of problems. But he hadn't, and she certainly wasn't going to bring it up. She planned to enjoy the moment—for however long that might be.

She and Gabe bought two plants—an ivy for the kitchen window and a palm for the dining room, and she went up in his helicopter as he showed clients several properties in the hill country. He wasn't showing them a house on a lot; the properties were tracts of many acres, mostly riverfront and with hefty prices. No wonder he lived so high on the hog. His commissions must be plenty.

He spent the nights at her house—at least the first part of it. He always left by midnight. "Small town," he said, and that was enough of an explanation. J.J. and Frank used to say that half of Naconiche timed how long their cars were outside when they were courting Mary Beth and Carrie. Not that she and Gabe were courting. They were simply having a lovely affair that might or might not turn into something more in a year or two.

Her creative writing instructor complimented her on her story about the Outlaw family and encouraged her to read it to the class. It wasn't fiction, but they seemed to find it interesting.

After class, Steve had said, "Your story was really good. You ought to think about doing some freelance magazine articles."

Hmm. Something to consider. Could one make a living doing that?

A bowl she'd made in ceramics class came out of the kiln looking halfway decent, its lopsided shape giving it character, the instructor said. It was a couple of shades of turquoise and brown with a streak of red that accidentally matched her couch. It was kind of odd-looking, but she put three decorative vine balls in it, set it on an end table and declared it a work of art. Gabe was appropriately complimentary. Bless his heart, as her mother would say.

On Thursday morning she picked up Skye for yoga class, and afterward she, Skye and Sally got their lattes to go and went to Belle's house to drink them.

"I've been dying to see your place," Skye said when they walked in. "I love it. It's so open and airy and colorful. And Mother's paintings are perfect." With Gus beside her and Belle and Sally trailing after her, Skye strolled through the house complimenting this thing and that. "You have plenty of room, but it's still cozy. What are you going to do with the extra bedroom?"

"That will be my office/library. My brother Sam is bringing the rest of my things this weekend."

"Is Sam the Texas Ranger?" Sally asked.

"He's the one."

"Well, I think your place is just great," Skye said. "Except for one thing."

Sally cocked an eyebrow, and Belle asked, "What's that?"

"You don't have much of a security system."

"The windows all have double locks, and I have a dead bolt."

"You really should have an alarm system," Skye said. "I don't like to think of you here alone without one."

"That's a good idea, Skye. I'll think about it."

"You should have a dog at least."

"I don't think my landlord allows pets except for maybe goldfish."

Sally grinned. "Can you get attack fish?"

"Maybe piranha," Skye said, and they all laughed.

Their coffees finished, Sally left to run errands, and Belle drove Skye home.

"I do like your town house and what you're doing with it. I can tell you're excited to have your own place and your own things."

"I am. I loved staying with all of you, but I'm a pretty independent sort. I enjoy my own space, and decorating it the way I like is fun."

Gabe was sitting on the porch when they drove up. He waved and walked out to the car as Skye said goodbye and hurried into the house to change. "Want to go to lunch with us?"

"Thanks, but I can't. I have an appointment this afternoon in San Marcos, and I need to go home and dress first."

"I have a business meeting tonight. I'll call you if it's not too late when I get out."

"Okay."

He bent down and gave her a kiss. He would have lingered, but she said, "Down, boy. Your mother is looking."

He glanced over his shoulder at Flora waving from the porch. "I thought she'd already left for her circle luncheon."

Flora hurried out to the car. "I only have a second, but I'm eager to see your new house. Do you have some time tomorrow?"

"Sure," Belle said. "Why don't you come by in the morning?"

"I'd love to. I have to run now. I'm late, and Winnie will kill me if I'm not there to give my report." She fluttered her fingers and hurried back into the house.

After ceramics class the day before, she, the Culbertson sisters and Steve had been brainstorming careers for Belle. Some of them were pretty funny, but everybody agreed that seeing a vocational counselor would be a good move.

"I don't think we have one in town," Alma had said. "At least not one in private practice."

"I talked to a great guy at the university in San Marcos," Steve said. "I'll call and get a referral for somebody in private practice if you want me to."

She did, and he had. She got the names of two people in Austin and one in San Marcos. Since it was closer, she opted for the one in San Marcos. The first appointment was for Thursday afternoon and would include an initial interview and several hours of testing and questionnaires. Her fingers were crossed that this might be the answer to her dilemma.

WHEN SHE'D RETURNED home that evening, she'd been mentally and physically bushed. Even thought the questions had a different focus, the test battery had been as extensive as that she'd done for the FBI. And as taxing. She was glad Gabe had a meeting and didn't make it by.

At ten o'clock sharp on Friday morning, Belle's doorbell rang. She opened it to find Flora with a lovely, earth-toned bud vase that she recognized as a fine piece of Charlie Walker's pottery.

Flora handed the vase to her. "I thought this might find a home here with you."

"It's beautiful, Flora. Thank you, but you've given me too much already."

"Oh, fiddle, how do a few old paintings and a vase compare to what you've brought to our family? To see Gabe so happy and Skye venturing out with friends her own age are like miracles to me. Oh, I like where you've placed the paintings. The poppies are perfect for the dining area and they bring the red to that side of the room."

"I still have to get frames for them, but I couldn't wait to see the paintings up. I'll be the envy of the town. Ready for coffee?"

"Yes, but I'd like to see your house first."

"That will only take two minutes," Belle said, "and I'm afraid that I'll have to serve your coffee in a foam cup until my brother gets here tomorrow with my dishes. The bedroom is through here."

"Foam doesn't matter to me, but I wish I'd known you were without cups, I would have brought you a set of Charlie's mugs. Oh, your bedspread is lovely."

"Garage sale bargain."

"You're joking. It's beautiful. Gabe's father and I used to go to flea markets and garage sales all the time, but I haven't been to one in years. They were always lots of fun. Your house is just darling," Flora said when they ended the tour in the kitchen.

"Thanks," Belle said, putting a plate of miniature bran muffins in the microwave to heat while she poured coffee and set the cups on a tray.

"That tray is so cute. Don't tell me you got that at a garage sale."

Belle grinned. "I did. A dollar fifty."

"Get out!"

"I did." She added napkins and muffins to the tray and took it to the dining table, where Flora demanded a blow-by-blow description of her bargain-hunting experience.

"That sounds like such fun. Sometimes it's a real bore to rattle around in that big old house that somebody else decorated—down to the color-coordinated toilet paper in my bathroom."

Belle almost spewed out her coffee, but she stayed cool. "Oh?"

"Yes. I want to talk to you about something, Belle. It's something I don't want to discuss with my family yet, and you have such a sensible head on your shoulders."

"I might argue that last point, but I'm a good sounding board."

Flora pursed her lips in a pleased smile. "I'm going to buy the Firefly! That is, if you've definitely decided not to."

"No, I'm not going to buy it, and I think that's wonderful. What will you do about your painting?"

"I'll move my studio to the gallery. I think people will enjoy seeing an artist at work. And I can hire part-time help if I need to. I need to be out and about with folks. Being a recluse is not my nature."

Flora grew more excited and animated as she talked to Belle about her plans for the Firefly. All her ideas sounded great, but she wondered what Gabe would think. For sure, she wasn't going to be the one that brought it up.

"WHEN DO YOU GO BACK to the counselor for results?" Gabe asked as they walked from her place to the square on Friday night. They were having dinner, then going dancing again at Fancy's.

"Next Friday morning. As I recall, an interest test I had in high school suggested that I had a lot in common with funeral directors. I hope this one is better."

Gabe hooked his arm around her neck. "Oh, I don't know, we could probably use another mortician in town."

"Bite your tongue, buster. Steve said that his counselor was very helpful to him."

"*Steve* said. I'm hearing a lot of '*Steve* saids.' Do you have a crush on that guy?"

Belle chuckled. "I might. He's a younger man, you know."

"I may have to pluck out my gray hairs and challenge him to spit wads at thirty paces."

"You don't have any gray hairs, and you know very well that Steve and I are just good friends. I like him."

"I know." He kept his arm hooked around her neck as they walked and drew her close for a kiss on the cheek. "He's a decent kid who's had some tough breaks."

They had a nice dinner and a fun evening dancing. They ran into Sally and Tim Olds at Fancy's and shared a table with them. Belle danced and laughed and talked and was still giddy when they left for home. They harmonized on a Brooks and

Dunn song as they walked. Rather, Gabe tried to harmonize. She caterwauled as usual. Thankfully, she forgot most of the words and had to content herself with humming. She was a better hummer than a singer.

Their lovemaking, often intense, had a playful, giddy element to it as well. They romped and made funny noises on each other's bodies and rolled off the bed laughing. Gabe was like no man she'd ever met. How had she ever thought she was in love with Matt?

She snuggled close to Gabe, content to sleep in his arms.

The doorbell rang.

Belle sat up and saw the bed beside her empty and daylight streaming in between the blinds. She pulled on her jeans and shirt from their heap on the floor, finger-combed her wild mop and went to the door barefoot.

Gabe, already dressed and his hair tamed, beat her there.

It was Sam.

Oh, crap!

Sam glanced at Gabe, then at her tell-all appearance, then scowled at Gabe. "What the hell are you doing here?"

"Fine, thank you, Sam. I'm here to help you unload Belle's stuff. I've got coffee ready to pour while Belle's been getting her beauty sleep."

"Gabe," Sam said, "I love you like a brother, but if you hurt her, I'll break both your legs and every finger you have."

"I understand. I feel the same about my sister."

"Yeah, but I've got three more just like me ready to show up on your doorstep. Let me go tell the guys this is the place. Morning, Belle." He tugged at the brim of his ball cap and trotted off, leaving Belle sputtering.

"What time is it?" Belle asked.

"Ten minutes after ten."

"Why did you let me sleep so long?" she asked. "And moreover, why are you still here?"

"I let you sleep because you were tired, and I went and got a thermos of coffee because your pot only makes a little bit. I got a couple of dozen donuts, too. I took your extra key."

Belle threw up her arms. "I'm going to brush my teeth."

By the time she emerged from the bathroom with clean teeth, glossed lips and tamed hair, Gabe, Sam and his two buddies were sitting at the dining table drinking coffee and scarfing down donuts.

"I hope you saved some for me," she said.

All the men stood. "We did," Gabe said. "Suki sent enough coffee for us and half the city council."

Sam introduced Luke and Don, two of his Ranger buddies. "Get your coffee, and we'll bring in your stuff."

"Works for me."

In twenty minutes, the men had all her stuff unloaded, her desk, bookcases and file cabinet set up in the office; her TV was in the armoire and hooked up to the cable, and all the other boxes were disbursed to various rooms to be unpacked later.

"If you guys ever leave the Rangers, you could start a moving company. How can I repay you?"

"Sam's already taken care of that," Luke said.

"Yeah," Don said. "We each get a free week at the lake house."

Sam gave her the keys to her SUV and a big hug. "You take care of yourself, Ding-dong. Call me if you need some legs broken."

Belle hugged her youngest brother fiercely. "I do my own

leg-breaking, baby buzzer." After she said her goodbyes, she stood outside and waved as Sam and Luke drove off in the moving truck with Don following in a black pickup.

Gabe stepped behind her and put his hands on her shoulders.

"You did that on purpose, didn't you?" she said.

"Did what, babe?"

"If you call me 'babe' again, *I'll* break all your fingers. And you know very well *what*. You hung around so Sam would think we're sleeping together."

"But, Belle, we *are* sleeping together."

"No, we aren't. Name one time that we've actually slept," she said, bursting into laughter.

He goosed her in the ribs, she goosed back, and he chased her into the house with him laughing and her squealing, "Don't, don't!"

One thing led to another, and it was well after noon before they got around to unpacking the boxes.

Chapter Nineteen

On the following Friday, Belle walked into the restaurant on the square where she was meeting Gabe for lunch. He stood and waved her over to a table where iced tea and a menu were waiting for her.

"How did your counseling session go?" Gabe asked.

"Well, I think. I got copies of all my reports, and we talked some. What are you having?"

"Ribs."

"I'm going for broke again. I'll have the chicken-fried steak special," she told the waitress, who wrote down their orders and hurried away.

"What did you talk about?"

"Well, in general, she suggested that I might want to look at careers that allowed me a certain amount of independence, a leadership role—seems I'm the bossy type—and something that involves service as well as creativity and challenge. Funeral director came up again."

Gabe grinned. "I was going to suggest that you might run for president. Or at least mayor."

"No politics for me. I need something that allows me time alone as well as time with others."

"You could teach."

"Teach what? I don't have any credentials. And besides, school politics would drive me nuts. I have a whole folder of job descriptions that fit my profile, and I'm sure I'll find something that interests me that I haven't even thought of. I'm hoping so anyhow."

At the next table, a burly man in overalls and a gimmie cap called out, "Hey, Lester, I didn't like that editorial you ran in Wednesday's paper worth a damn."

"Too bad, Bud," a salty-looking gray-haired man said as he walked toward the table. "Why don't you write a letter to the editor? Or better yet, buy the *Star*. I'm putting it up for sale."

Belle's ears perked up.

"You're bull-shootin' me," Bud said.

"Nope. Sue Nell and I have decided to sell the paper and move to Corpus Christi to be closer to our grandkids."

"Lester, we'll hate to lose you," Gabe said, joining the conversation. "When are you leaving?"

Lester moved toward Gabe, who introduced him to Belle as owner and publisher of the *Wimberley Star*. "I'm not sure. We just decided this week. We're not getting any younger, and Sue Nell's allergies are really giving her a fit. The doctor said the coast would be better for her, and what better place to be than near our two grandchildren?"

"Do you have a buyer?" Belle asked.

"No. We haven't made a formal announcement yet, but I've been putting out some feelers." He nodded to her. "Nice to meet you, Belle. Gabe, you might spread the word a little."

"I'll do that, Lester."

After the newspaper man left, Gabe said, "Know anything about newspapers?"

"Does being editor of my high school paper count? And I was on the staff of the college paper my last two years there. Why?"

"Maybe running a paper would fit your job description."

"The thought struck me, too. I'll have to consider it. That's a little more serious than buying an art gallery."

"But it's also more of a challenge."

BELLE COULDN'T GET the idea out of her head. The more she read in her profile, the more the job seemed to fit. Excitement started building in her. It would be a challenge all right. But what did she know about running a real newspaper?

Next to nothing. But she could learn.

How much would this venture cost? That might shoot down the proposition immediately. She had lots of questions, questions that only Lester Franks could answer. Only one way to solve that problem. She called him at the paper and made an appointment to see him the following day.

"I'M NOT A JOURNALIST," Belle said. "My only newspaper experience is on my high school and college papers."

"Same issues here as there," Lester said, "except on a bigger scale. You have to have personnel, content, advertising, production and distribution. Those systems are already in place with the *Star*. In fact, I'd urge that a new owner keep the present personnel in place at least for a while."

They talked for over two hours and toured the *Star*'s facilities, which occupied a building on a side street off the square. Since the paper was closed on weekends, no one was around, but she got a good overview of things. They discussed not only day-to-day operations, but also financial considerations. Bottom line: the paper was in the black, and she could swing the purchase price since Lester wanted to finance the sale himself.

Belle gathered up the papers Lester offered, stood and shook his hand. "Let me have some time to think about this and discuss it with my advisors, and I'll get back to you next week. And, in fact, I'd like to spend a day or two in the offices before I decide to see if I like being a publisher."

"Fair enough. We open Monday morning at eight-thirty. And if you decide you want to buy the paper, I would hang around for a while and show you the ropes. Shoot, I was green as grass when I started the *Star*. You'll catch on quick enough." He grinned. "It's not exactly the *New York Times*."

Maybe not, Belle thought, but with that attitude, she'd bet there's plenty of room to work on closing the gap.

As soon as she left, Belle called Gabe. "You have time for a cup of coffee? I just had a meeting with Lester Franks, and I need to meet with my advisors."

"Sure. Who are your advisors?"

"You and me."

He chuckled. "Tell you what. I have an even better idea. Pack an overnight bag, and we'll drive down to San Antonio and take side roads to enjoy the bluebonnets."

"Gabe, I'm from Texas, remember? I've seen bluebonnets all my life, and they've been blooming for a week. I need some help making a momentous decision, not traipsing around the countryside rhapsodizing over wildflowers."

"Don't go stompin' on baby ducks, Belle, my love. The two activities aren't mutually exclusive. I can talk and drive. Usually get my best thinking done when I drive. I'll pick you up in half an hour. Bring a camera. And a pretty dress for dinner."

He hung up before she could argue.

Although she grumbled about it, Belle was ready when Gabe arrived, and they were soon on the road, headed for San Antonio.

"Deal sounds good, huh?" Gabe asked.

"You tell me." She outlined her meeting with Lester. That took about ten miles.

He didn't say anything for a few minutes. Instead, he turned off onto a country lane and stopped. She studied his face, trying to get a reading on his thoughts. "Well?" she finally asked.

"Look," he said, motioning ahead of them.

Irritated by his inattention to her concerns, she turned and looked to where he pointed.

Her breath caught.

On both sides of the dirt lane, and even in the space between the ruts, for as far as she could see was a carpet of blue. She'd seen bluebonnets all her life, had seen magnificent paintings and photographs of every kind, but she'd never seen anything quite like this. These were *Bluebonnets* with a capital *B*.

She grabbed her camera and jumped from the car.

At first she simply soaked up the beauty of the fields on both sides of an old barbed wire fence, its gnarled fence posts looking like millions she'd seen in East Texas.

"I've never seen so many in one place," she said. "They're spectacular."

"They seem to like it here. They thrive in the alkaline soil."

"East Texas has beautiful wildflowers, too, including blue-bonnets, but the soil is more acid, better suited for dogwood, pine trees and azaleas, which I don't ever see much around here." She snapped picture after picture.

"Save some film," Gabe said.

"Nothing could be better than this."

"Just wait."

Back in the car, he followed the meandering road for several miles, then pulled to a stop on a shaded bluff.

"I don't see anything."

He smiled. "You will." He got out of the car, and she followed. It was a scenic spot, but nothing like the site they'd seen earlier. He popped the trunk, handed her a quilt and retrieved an insulated carrier. "Come on," he said, offering his hand.

He led her through a stand of trees to a gently sloping path down the hill. "What about this?"

Her breath left her again as they walked through what seemed like acres and acres of bluebonnets that ran down a gully, across a field and up a gently rolling hill. The sight was even more awesome than the last one. He stopped and spread the quilt she carried over the flowers.

"Oh, don't! You'll crush them."

He laughed. "They're tough. And the property owner won't mind."

"How do you know?" she asked. Then she realized what he was saying. "You own this piece of heaven?"

"I do."

"If this were mine, I would pitch a tent and live here the whole season."

He locked his arms around her waist and looked down at her. "Marry me, and I'll give it to you as a wedding present."

Stunned, she could only look up at him and blink. No words came.

He laughed and kissed her. "That's the first time I've seen you speechless. Sit down and we'll have some chicken."

"How can you drop a bomb like that and then blithely eat a drumstick?"

"Because I'm quick of mind and nimble of foot, and I have sense enough to know when to beat a tactical retreat." He sat down and unzipped the insulated bag.

"Forget doing the fast shuffle." She lowered herself to sit cross-legged facing him. "Gabe, I'm not nearly ready to talk about marrying anybody. I may never be."

"Never?"

"Well, not for a long time."

"Okay. You want a breast or a thigh?"

"Boy, that was easy," she said, feeling slightly miffed.

"I understand your feelings, and I didn't mean to say anything. It just slipped out of my mouth before I thought. Don't worry about it. Want some potato salad?"

She tried to pursue the subject, but he was determined to move on, so she gave up and ate.

When they'd finished with their meal, Gabe stretched out, his head in her lap. She leaned back on her hands and surveyed the undulating sea of blue that surrounded her. If she could have carried a tune, she would have pretended that she was Julie Andrews coming over the hill and singing "The Sound of Music." She had loved that movie since she was a little girl and must have watched the video a thousand times, enough so that her brothers groaned when she begged to watch it again. This place evoked the same sort of wondrous feeling as that opening scene did.

Her spirit simply soared here.

Gabe picked a flower and tickled her nose with it. "You look as if you're a million miles away."

"I am. I'm in the Alps."

"Ever been there?"

"Not yet."

He tucked the bluebonnet behind her ear, then pulled her mouth down to his.

She'd never made love in a field of flowers.

It was glorious.

THEY DISCUSSED her purchasing the *Star* all the way to San Antonio. The prospects sounded better and better. Gabe had made reservations at a lovely hotel on the Riverwalk, and after they checked in, he looked through the papers that Lester had given her. She explained about the financing deal.

"Can you swing that comfortably?" he asked. "Or would you like to take on a partner? I'd be willing."

"I'd rather do it by myself." She explained about her oil-lease money. "I can put profits into paying off the debt and covering any expansion plans for a while. I might not get rich, but in a couple of years I should have an adequate living. And I think I'll like it."

"I hope so. Seems to me that the only thing yet to do is spend a few days at the paper and see if it appeals to you."

"I report first thing Monday morning."

"Great. Let's go down and take a stroll along the River-walk. Have you ever been in one of the paddle boats there?"

"Nope. And I haven't been to the Alamo since I was sixteen."

They made the Alamo first, then went back and walked along the river. The area had been turned into a lovely spot several years ago, beautified and developed with hotels, restaurants and a variety of quaint shops. She bought candles in one shop and napkin rings in another.

Foot bridges crossed the narrow river, and they looked over the railings of one and watched a paddle boat filled with tourists pass under them.

"Want to give it a try?"

"Sure."

At the landing they caught the first one by and rode down the river until the lights began to come on at dusk, then went back to the hotel.

Upstairs, Gabe took a shower, shaved and turned over the bathroom to Belle. He quickly dressed, except for his suit coat, and brushed his hair. He'd almost blown it when he'd mentioned marriage this afternoon. He wanted to kick himself. He was so sure of what he wanted that he'd failed to remember that she was still recovering from a traumatic divorce. Because he knew they were perfect together didn't mean that she'd realized it yet.

When she opened the door a few minutes later, he turned and his heart skipped a beat. She wore a two piece dress that looked cloud-soft and was the exact color of bluebonnets.

"You look beautiful," Gabe said. "More beautiful than all the bluebonnets in Texas. Stunning."

"Thank you." She kissed his cheek. "You're good for a woman's ego."

"And you're good for a man's. I'll be the envy of every man in the restaurant. Maybe we should order room service."

"Bite your tongue, big guy. I'm primed for lobster at the fancy place upstairs."

He pulled on his coat and offered his arm. "Anything your heart desires is yours."

Chapter Twenty

Belle had to cancel her ceramics class, but at 8:30 a.m. on Monday morning, she reported to the *Wimberley Star*. By 5:30 p.m. that afternoon, she thought she was on to something with this idea of buying the paper. By the time the Wednesday issue hit the stands and driveways of the area, she was throwing around terms like stringer, byline, tearsheet and newshole that she ordinarily didn't use, let alone know what some of them meant. She even knew what sidebars and jumplines were. She always figured that learning the lingo in any situation was half the battle.

Also, she was getting the lowdown about the sacred cows in Wimberley—those people or issues that were normally avoided because of the individual's prominence or the issue's sensitivity—and feeling her hackles rise about the whole concept. What about free press?

Lester shot down her sanctimonious stance when he reminded her that Skye Walker was one of the sacred cows.

"How so?"

"You know about her kidnapping several years ago?" he asked.

Belle nodded. She'd never discussed the circumstances in great detail with Gabe, nor had she researched it on the Internet as she'd intended. It seemed an inappropriate invasion of Skye's privacy.

"So do most people around here. The old-timers anyhow. The *Wimberley Star* never printed any of the gory details about her abduction. In the first place, the *Star*'s not into sensational journalism. We leave that to the big-city papers. And we've stayed away from the story. Everybody in town back then saw pictures of that homemade coffin she was buried alive in. Photographs were splashed across the front pages of the city papers showing that grave they dug up, but we dang sure didn't print any. We had a bare bone report at the time."

"Out of respect for the family," Belle said. "I see."

And she did. When Lester mentioned the coffin, she remembered the case. She'd been in law school when it happened, and the incident had been the talk of the campus. A coed at A&M had been kidnapped and held for ransom. It had been one of a string of abductions by the "coed kidnapper" in universities across Texas that had spooked college women and had them travelling everywhere in groups. Several young women had been taken; their families had paid ransoms, but they were never seen again. Except the one from A&M. Her dog's incessant barking and digging had led to the discovery of the plywood box she'd been buried in.

Dear God. That had been Skye.

No wonder she had security issues.

No wonder Gabe was so protective. Could she respect him if he weren't? Her brothers would have done no less.

When she and Gabe were alone together that night, she confronted him about Skye's ordeal. "Why haven't you told me about it before? She's told me more than you have."

"A couple of reasons." He stood and started jingling the coins in his pocket, a sure sign he was nervous.

"Like what?"

"We all like to put the past out of our minds as much as we can. It was a traumatic time in Skye's life, in the whole family's life. If it hadn't been for Kaiser, we…we would have been like those other families who never got their sisters and daughters back."

"I can understand that. I've worked kidnapping cases. It must have been terrible for you and Flora."

He nodded, but the coins kept jingling, and he turned to stare out the window of her living room, though it was dark outside.

"Is there something else? Some other reason you've avoided the subject?"

Gabe turned around and looked at her, his expression tortured. Her first instinct was to hurry to him, gather him into her arms and comfort him. She kept her seat. He had something crucial to say, and she had to wait until he said it.

"I don't think I ever told you why Lisa and I split up."

"No."

He turned back and stared out the window. "When Charlie was dying, he made me promise that I would always look out for Flora and Skye. I swore to him the day before he died that I would. Always. But I screwed up. I let Flora marry a sorry bastard who almost destroyed her emotionally, and I let Skye nearly get killed."

"Gabe, Skye and your mother were grown women who made their own choices. You weren't responsible for what happened to them."

"I've tried to tell myself that, but I don't really believe it. I didn't take my vow seriously enough, and I've been given a second chance. I don't intend to fall down on the job this time."

"You feel guilty. Maybe unreasonably guilty, but guilty anyhow."

"Yes. I have to do everything in my power to look out for them so that won't happen again. That's my first priority. It has to be."

She nodded. "I understand." And she did. It sounded excessive and obsessive, but she understood. "What does this have to do with Lisa?"

"She said that she refused to live in a house ruled by two neurotic women. She wanted them gone. It came down to either I kicked them out or she left. I had to choose."

"And you didn't choose her?"

"No. I couldn't do that and live with myself as a man."

"Are you still in love with Lisa?"

Gabe looked horrified. "Good God, no! I know now that I never was. Not really. I love you. Don't you know that by now? I'm crazy, mad, can't-think-straight in love with you."

"And your problem is?"

The coins started jingling again.

"Do you think I'm like Lisa?"

"You're *nothing* like Lisa."

"But you think I might try to make you toss your mother and sister out on the street?"

He didn't say anything for what seemed like a week, and she felt a guilt pang or two herself. She had groused to herself about independence and privacy and living in a zoo at Gabe's. Her concerns seemed petty now. She would have respected Gabe less if he'd shirked his responsibility and kicked his family out.

Belle stood then and went to him. She wrapped her arms around him and rested her head on his shoulder. "I'm glad to hear that Lisa was a first-class bitch."

She felt Gabe's shoulders relax.

"People who love each other find solutions to their problems and work things out," she said, rubbing his back. "Very little is insurmountable with love and compromise."

He hugged her fiercely. "God, I love you. What did I ever do to deserve someone like you?"

"You came to my rescue in your helicopter. I thought you were an angel the first time I ever saw you." She grinned. "Now I know you're a devil."

He laughed.

"Want to know the biggest thing that bothers me about your household?"

"What?"

"Knowing that Lisa picked out everything in it."

"I'll get a bulldozer first thing in the morning, shove every stick of furniture out of the place and burn it."

Belle chuckled. "Save your matches for a while."

"Does this mean that now isn't the time to propose again?"

"Not yet." She stroked the face that she had grown to love in such a short time and kissed him. "Try me again in a few months."

BELLE SPENT the next few weeks discovering that she loved the newspaper business almost as much as she loved Gabe. By the time the bluebonnets faded, she and Lester Franks had made a deal. Part of that deal was that he would stay on until she felt comfortable in her duties. She even had a couple of seminars lined up to learn more about the latest innovations, especially in online services, a great avenue for growth.

"I can't believe it!" she told Gabe, waving the papers she'd signed in the lawyer's office. "I'm a newspaper publisher!" She hugged him. "It must be destiny. Starr is my middle name."

Gabe groaned at her pun, then laughed and whirled her around. "I'm happy for you, Miss Belle, love. What exciting thing shall we do to celebrate?"

"Want to go play bingo tonight?"

"If you want, but I was thinking of something more formal and festive—like throwing a party."

"Sounds fabulous. Where? When?"

"How about the country club? In two weeks."

"You're on!"

THE PARTY WAS a huge success. Everybody was there. Well, not everybody, but all the *Star* staff and the new friends she'd made in town attended. Her parents and Cole had made the trip down from Naconiche, and Sam had come from San Antonio. Even Skye was there in a new dress that made her look like a fairy princess—along with an assortment of guards posted around the room—and Flora was in her element introducing the Outlaws to Mason Perdue, the Culbertsons, Bea McClure and Sally and Tim Olds.

Steve was there in a new tie, and Dr. Hamilton sought out Cole to talk with. Belle was only sorry that the timing was terrible for Mary Beth and Carrie. Since it was so late in their pregnancies, Kelly wouldn't let them travel, especially knowing now that Mary Beth was having twins. And naturally J.J. and Frank stayed home with their wives, and Kelly stayed in Naconiche on the off-chance that either of them went into labor.

Gabe put his arm around her waist. "Aren't you having a good time?"

"I'm having a wonderful time," she said. "I'm only sorry that all my family couldn't be here."

"We'll have another party after the babies are born." He glanced toward the door. "Who are those big guys coming in?"

Belle looked over to see two men who stood half a head or more taller than those around them. She brightened. "It's J.J. and Frank. Come on." She dragged Gabe across the room after her.

"Hey there, baby sister," J.J. said.

"Surprise," Frank said.

"How did you two get here?"

"Somebody named Gabe Burrell chartered a plane and loaded Frank and me on it," J.J. said, kissing her cheek.

"Kelly, Mary Beth, Carrie and all the kids are having their own party while we're gone for a couple of hours," Frank said. "They sent this." He handed her a gift-wrapped box.

"Oh, guys, this is Gabe. Gabe, this is J.J. and Frank."

Gabe shook hands with them, and Sam and Cole soon found their way over. The men talked while Belle opened the gift.

It was a handsome wooden desk sign with an engraved brass plate. *Belle Starr Outlaw. Publisher.*

"Oh, it's wonderful! Thank you." She hugged everybody again, even Gabe. "Thank you for sending a plane. You're a dear, sweet man."

"He's a pretty good guy," Cole said, mostly to his brothers. "I think he's a keeper."

"Didn't I tell you?" Sam said.

Sam cut out in a couple of minutes, and Belle glanced around for him and saw him talking to Skye. He looked a little smitten himself, and Skye was laughing. Belle wondered what had happened to Julie, the one he'd been engaged to last Christmas. She hadn't heard him mention her. She shrugged and turned back to the party.

After a couple of hours, it was time for J.J. and Frank to leave, and Cole decided to hitch a ride back with them on the plane. Her parents were staying at Gabe's house and planned to extend their stay for another day or two to see the town and visit.

Belle hugged her brothers before they left, and J.J. whispered in her ear, "I like this one. But take your time."

She and Gabe said goodbyes to the other guests as the crowd gradually dwindled until only the two of them were left.

"It was a wonderful party," Belle said. "Thank you."

"My pleasure." He kissed her tenderly, then plucked two glasses of wine from a tray and handed one to her. "I love you, you know."

"And I love you, too."

His face lit up. "You do?"

"I do. More than I ever thought possible." She touched her glass to his. "Let's drink to new beginnings, and to the future."

"To our future."

She smiled. "Blow, Gabriel, blow."

* * * * *

Watch for the next book in the
TEXAS OUTLAWS *series,*
Sam and Skye's story, THE TEXAS RANGER,
coming in May 2007,
only from Harlequin American Romance.

*Experience entertaining women's fiction about rediscovery
and reconnection—warm, compelling stories
that are relevant for every woman
who has wondered "What's next?" in their lives.
After all, there's the life you planned.
And there's what comes next.*

*Turn the page for a sneak preview
of a new book from Harlequin NEXT.*

*CONFESSIONS OF A NOT-SO-DEAD LIBIDO
by Peggy Webb*

*On sale November 2006,
wherever books are sold.*

My husband could see beauty in a mud puddle. Literally. "Look at that, Louise," he'd say after a heavy spring rain. "Have you ever seen so many amazing colors in mud?"

I'd look and see nothing except brown, but he'd pick up a stick and swirl the mud till the colors of the earth emerged, and all of a sudden I'd see the world through his eyes—extraordinary instead of mundane.

Roy was my mirror to life. Four years ago when he died, it cracked wide open, and I've been living a smashed-up, sleepwalking life ever since.

If he were here on this balmy August night I'd be sailing with him instead of baking cheese straws in preparation for Tuesday-night quilting club with Patsy. I'd be striving for sex appeal in Bermuda shorts and bare-toed sandals instead of opting for comfort in walking shoes and a twill skirt with enough elastic around the waist to make allowances for two helpings of lemon-cream pie.

Not that I mind Patsy. Just the opposite. I love her. She's the only person besides Roy who creates wonder wherever she goes. (She creates mayhem, too, but we won't get into that.) She's my mirror now, as well as my compass.

Of course, I have my daughter, Diana, but I refuse to be the kind of mother who defines herself through her children. Besides, she has her own life now, a husband and a baby on the way.

I slide the last cheese straws into the oven and then go into my office and open e-mail.

From: "Miss Sass" <patsyleslie@hotmail.com>
To: "The Lady" <louisejernigan@yahoo.com>
Sent: Tuesday, August 15, 6:00 PM
Subject: Dangerous Tonight
Hey Lady,
I'm feeling dangerous tonight. Hot to trot, if you know what I mean. Or can you even remember? Look out, bridge club, here I come. I'm liable to end up dancing on the tables instead of bidding three spades. Whose turn is it to drive, anyhow? Mine or thine?
XOXOX
Patsy
P.S. Lord, how did we end up in a club with no men?

This e-mail is typical "Patsy." She's the only person I know who makes me laugh all the time. I guess that's why I e-mail her about ten times a day. She lives right next door, but e-mail satisfies my urge to be instantly and constantly in touch with her without having to interrupt the flow of my life. Sometimes we even save the good stuff for e-mail.

From: "The Lady" <louisejernigan@yahoo.com>
To: "Miss Sass" <patsyleslie@hotmail.com>
Sent: Tuesday, August 15, 6:10 PM
Subject: Re: Dangerous Tonight

So, what else is new, Miss Sass? You're always dangerous. If you had a weapon, you'd be lethal.

Hugs,

Louise

P.S. What's this about men? I thought you said your libido was dead?

I press Send then wait. Her reply is almost instantaneous.

From: "Miss Sass" <patsyleslie@hotmail.com>
To: "The Lady" <louisejernigan@yahoo.com>
Sent: Tuesday, August 15, 6:12 PM
Subject: Re: Dangerous Tonight

Ha! If I had a *brain* I'd be lethal.

And I said my libido was in hibernation, not DEAD!

Jeez, Louise!!!!!

P

Patsy loves to have the last word, so I shut off my computer.

* * * * *

*Want to find out what happens to their friendship
when Patsy and Louise both find the perfect man?*

*Don't miss
CONFESSIONS OF A NOT-SO-DEAD LIBIDO
by Peggy Webb,
coming to Harlequin NEXT
in November 2006.*

Introducing...

n o c t u r n e™

**a dark and sexy new
paranormal romance line
from Silhouette Books.**

USA TODAY bestselling author

LINDSAY McKENNA
UNFORGIVEN

KATHLEEN KORBEL
DANGEROUS TEMPTATION

*Launching October 2006,
wherever books are sold.*

SAVE UP TO $30! SIGN UP TODAY!

INSIDE *Romance*

The complete guide to your favorite
Harlequin®, Silhouette® and Love Inspired® books.

✓ Newsletter ABSOLUTELY FREE! No purchase necessary.

✓ Valuable coupons for future purchases of Harlequin,
  Silhouette and Love Inspired books in every issue!

✓ Special excerpts & previews in each issue. Learn about all
  the hottest titles before they arrive in stores.

✓ No hassle—mailed directly to your door!

✓ Comes complete with a handy shopping checklist
  so you won't miss out on any titles.

- -

SIGN ME UP TO RECEIVE INSIDE ROMANCE
ABSOLUTELY FREE
(Please print clearly)

Name

Address

City/Town   State/Province   Zip/Postal Code

(098 KKM EJL9)

Please mail this form to:
In the U.S.A.: Inside Romance, P.O. Box 9057, Buffalo, NY 14269-9057
In Canada: Inside Romance, P.O. Box 622, Fort Erie, ON L2A 5X3
OR visit http://www.eHarlequin.com/insideromance

IRNBPA06R   ® and ™ are trademarks owned and used by the trademark owner and/or its licensee.

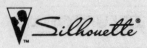

REQUEST YOUR FREE BOOKS!
2 FREE NOVELS PLUS 2
FREE GIFTS!

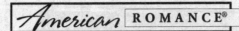

American ROMANCE®

Heart, Home & Happiness!

YES! Please send me 2 FREE Harlequin American Romance® novels and my 2 FREE gifts. After receiving them, if I don't wish to receive any more books, I can return the shipping statement marked "cancel." If I don't cancel, I will receive 4 brand-new novels every month and be billed just $4.24 per book in the U.S., or $4.99 per book in Canada, plus 25¢ shipping and handling per book and applicable taxes, if any*. That's a savings of close to 15% off the cover price! I understand that accepting the 2 free books and gifts places me under no obligation to buy anything. I can always return a shipment and cancel at any time. Even if I never buy another book from Harlequin, the two free books and gifts are mine to keep forever.

154 HDN EEZK   354 HDN EEZV

Name _____ (PLEASE PRINT)

Address _____ Apt. #

City _____ State/Prov. _____ Zip/Postal Code

Signature (if under 18, a parent or guardian must sign)

Mail to the Harlequin Reader Service®:

IN U.S.A.	IN CANADA
P.O. Box 1867	P.O. Box 609
Buffalo, NY	Fort Erie, Ontario
14240-1867	L2A 5X3

Not valid to current Harlequin American Romance subscribers.

Want to try two free books from another line?
Call 1-800-873-8635 or visit www.morefreebooks.com.

* Terms and prices subject to change without notice. NY residents add applicable sales tax. Canadian residents will be charged applicable provincial taxes and GST. This offer is limited to one order per household. All orders subject to approval. Credit or debit balances in a customer's account(s) may be offset by any other outstanding balance owed by or to the customer. Please allow 4 to 6 weeks for delivery.

HAR06

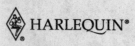

HARLEQUIN®

American **ROMANCE®**

COMING NEXT MONTH

#1137 THE CHRISTMAS TWINS by Tina Leonard
The Tulips Saloon

When Zach Forrester first meets Jessie Farnsworth she's in need of rescuing—and an attitude adjustment. After a passionate encounter, reason sets in and Zach realizes Jessie may be pregnant with his child. But can Zach's determination and Southern charm convince Jessie to let him into her heart in time for the holidays?

#1138 LONE STAR SANTA by Heather MacAllister

A false money-laundering charge sends Mitch Donner back to Mom and Dad's for the holidays. Kristen Zaleski is about to make it big in Hollywood—until an empty bank account lands her back in Sugar Land, Texas. Both sets of parents agree—it will take a Christmas miracle to get their kids out of the house. But is this too big a job, even for Santa?

#1139 THE QUIET CHILD by Debra Salonen
Sisters of the Silver Dollar

When her ex-fiancé asks Alex Radonovic to help his son, her first reaction is to refuse. After all, the child is proof of Mark's betrayal. But her heart goes out to the sad little boy, and she recalls her mother's prediction. *A child's laughter can heal a wounded heart, but first you have to heal the child.* By helping Braden, will she finally be able to forgive his father?

#1140 COURT ME, COWBOY by Barbara White Daille
Baby To Be

Miller men were unlucky in marriage. Or so Gabe thought until his ex, Melissa, came back to him in time for Christmas and gave him the most precious gift in the world. She was determined not to stay, but he was just as determined to change her mind—*before* she disappeared with his son....

www.eHarlequin.com